Beneath a Dark Moon

Beneath a Dark Moon

Lanny Green

VANTAGE PRESS
New York

Cover design by Susan Thomas

FIRST EDITION

Published by Vantage Press, Inc.
419 Park Ave. South, New York, NY 10016

Manufactured in the United States of America
ISBN: 978-0-533-15887-4

Library of Congress Catalog Card No.: 2007905985

0 9 8 7 6 5 4 3 2

Preface

It is the nature of saviors to be vague about their ability to save. It is also in the nature of people not to believe in them. It is a paradox of religion that the supposedly true prophets or saviors talk of works with faith, while the people ask for works before faith, therefore the savior must be a miracle worker as well.

Saviors tend to appeal to the "have nots," usually asking them to have even less; in essence he wants them to ask for nothing now but have faith in his works and do the work of the Lord and all will be given them in the afterlife. The people, however, have found a novel way to deal with this. They exude a great deal of faith, asking for the rewards promised them in the afterlife while working for whatever rewards they can acquire in this life.

Let's take for example perhaps the greatest savior of all time, Christ, who by the same token was the most vague of all the saviors. What can be more vague than the statement, "The meek shall inherit the earth." And what about the statement, "Give Caesar's things to Caesar but God's things to God." Where does one draw the distinction between which things belong to Caesar and which belongs to God? And if Caesar is considered a god then what does one do?

Now you may be asking what exactly does all this have to do with the story you are about to read? Probably nothing. However, if nothing else, what you should get out of all this is that it is in the nature of writers, like saviors, to be vague and the nature of their readers to have faith in their works.

Introduction

The carnage was the worst he had ever seen. As far as he could see there were wounded and dead lying in blood-colored pools of mud. The crying of the wounded and dying and the stench of blood and bile was overwhelming. The worst thing yet was the screaming of the horses. He had fought in many battles and always it was the same. Some baron attacking a neighboring kingdom because of a petty squabble over hunting rights, or some minor king with the ambition of expanding his kingdom. And always it was the peasants who invariably paid the price for their rulers' egos. But people, like animals, were stupid and they paid for that stupidity by dying for something they could not even share in.

He was a mercenary, he fought for money, so the reasons why were not important to him. His only concern was that he got paid. He was able to maintain a certain emotional detachment from all the senseless death, yet he had not quite gotten used to the screams of the animals who invariably got slaughtered along with the people in these wars. The screams of the horses and the anguished mews of the pack animals haunted him when he tried to sleep.

Jodell walked through the battlefield surveying the damage and shuddered. He had ridden into this valley in the early morning at the head of an army of twenty-thousand men against an opposing army of nearly twice that many and nearly all of them had been slaughtered. He could still hear the clanking of swords in the distance as the soldiers tracked down those who had tried to escape. The sun was starting to go down now as he made his way toward the large tent that was situated in the middle of their camp. Fires were starting to be lighted all over the camp; he could even smell the fragrance of spiced wine being heated, reminding him he had not eaten since early morning. His thoughts were interrupted by the sound of a voice weakly calling to him. There was a man lying in the shadows of a large tree, propped up against it. He was a large man probably well over six feet tall with huge arms and hands that clutched at a gaping wound in his abdomen. His long blonde hair was matted with mud and blood, his large blue eyes glazed over with pain. Jodell walked over to the man and stood looking down at him for a second. It had been a long time since he had last seen him. The man's voice was filled with pain as he spoke.

"Hello, my friend." Jodell could hear the gurgle of fluids in his lungs.

"Hello, Karle." Jodell greeted him, wincing at the acrid smell of bile. Karle smiled knowingly as Jodell reflexively covered his nose. "I know I do not smell so good right now, but then I never was too fond of bathing." He tried to laugh but broke into a gurgling cough forcing more blood to ooze from between his fingers. As his coughing subsided he spoke again.

"It has been a long time my friend, about ten years I would say. The last time I saw you, you were hightailing it out of that Thithian city on the coast. Had something to do with a lady of fairly extensive means if I remember correctly."

"That was a long time ago, I am suprised you still remember it," Jodell said. "The last I heard you were still south causing trouble. What brings you so far north?"

"You know me, always looking for new opportunities I guess. Ever since that bastard son of King Arghos took the throne in Tithe things have been rather bad for mercenaries.

I do not think he trusts us very much." Karle stopped as a wave of pain hit him.

"How did you allow this to happen?" Jodell indicated the wound in Karle's abdomen.

"Got careless I guess, let this young fellow get the drop on me. He cut me down before I knew what happened. He rather reminded me of you by the way. His technique was similar to yours: long fluid strokes and quick, too quick for me."

Jodell thought for a moment. "Yeah I know who you mean. Young kid with hair like yours. Rather thinly built for his height but fast with that axe of his but a little too impulsive with his attack."

"That sounds like him alright. Did he survive the battle?" Jodell reflexively rubbed the hilt of his sword and started to walk away as he answered.

"No."

Karle nodded his head in understanding. "Jodell," Karle's voice was lowered and sounded more strained. Jodell stopped and turned back to him. "I would appreciate it if you would do something for me, for old times sake if you will."

"What is it?" Jodell asked.

"I have a wife and kid. Kid will be eight in a month or so. Looks just like her mother, eyes so green they . . ." He stopped talking as another wave of pain hit him. "Anyway they are waiting for me in the old monastery in that town about six miles west of here. Obviously I will never make it back there now."

"What would you have me do?" Jodell asked already knowing what it would be.

"Collect my pay and take it to them for me." He handed Jodell a small piece of parchment. Jodell took it and slipped it into his pocket. "Instructions for the sergeant to give you the money." Jodell nodded his understanding.

"How much?" Jodell asked.

"Six hundred in gold."

"I only got four hundred," Jodell said.

"I insisted." Karle smiled as Jodell turned to walk away again. "One more thing before you go."

"What now?" Jodell asked without turning around this time. He was tired of seeing men die; tired of making men die.

"I would appreciate it if you would loan me your dagger. I seem to need to trim and clean my nails." Jodell knew he was being sarcastic. He knew what he wanted the dagger for. Karle's wounds were such that he could live for hours with the pain getting worse and worse by the minute. Jodell drew a dagger from his boot and flipped it to him.

"Thanks," Karle said as he hefted the dagger between blood caked fingers.

"Yeah," was all Jodell said as he walked away.

*   *   *

The commander's tent was full of activity with soldiers running in and out with reports. Jodell waited a few minutes to allow the traffic to die down a little before he entered. There were two guards stationed at the entrance, which stopped anyone wanting to enter the commander's tent.

"Hold and state your business." One of the guards barked out the words, lowering his spear at the same time. Jodell stopped and let out a sigh of annoyance.

"I wish to speak with the commander, please step aside." Jodell's tone was acid as he eyed the two guards.

"My orders are to admit no one except unit leaders."

"Look," Jodell pushed back his cloak he wore over his shoulders so that the guards could clearly see the hilt of his sword and spoke through clenched teeth. His tone belying his choice of words. "Please tell your commander that Jodell is here to see him and wants to see him now." The two guards looked at each other nervously. Jodell put his hand on his sword suggestively and shouted. "I said now."

The guards both jumped and nervously fingered their spears. Jodell slowly drew his sword from its scabbard. "I will not tell you again, not in words anyway," Jodell said as he shifted into a defensive stance. One of the guards immediately stuck his head inside the tent and mumbled a few words then turned back to Jodell.

"The commander will see you now," a little of his former bravado edging back into his voice. Jodell stepped closer and looked directly into his eyes. The guard looked back for a couple of seconds then looked away.

"Thank you, soldier," Jodell said as he stepped past him and into the tent.

The commander's tent was not lavish but it was comfortably furnished with soft pelt carpets and sturdy yet comfortable chairs. There was a large desk sitting in the middle of the tent, draped with parchments and stacks of papers. Behind him were other rooms which were curtained off. Jodell could sense movement from there and knew it was probably a female.

Jodell approached the huge desk and stood before it waiting to be acknowledged by the commander. He did not like this man very much and knew that the feelings were mutual. However, at this point, he did not care whether he was liked or not. He simply wanted to get paid so he could leave. He was not in the mood to be kept waiting.

"Sergeant," Jodell deliberately got the rank wrong because he knew it would get his attention. The commander looked up then his face flushing red with anger.

"How many times do I have to tell you it's commander?" He was clearly upset. Jodell was amused at just how red this little man could get. The commander was not a very imposing figure at five foot seven inches tall. His hair was bald on top and thinning everywhere else. He was fat with a huge paunch for a stomach and an ego to match. He was commander only because he was the king's brother-in-law.

"Commander, sergeant, whatever, it's all the same to me," Jodell said with a wave of his hand as if to dismiss the subject as trivial. He was amused to see that the little man got even redder. "My job here is done. You have a victory, so now I want to get paid as agreed; then I shall be on my way. Jodell could see the wheels of greed start to turn in the commander's eyes.

"Fine," the little man said as he made some pretense to be looking for something on his desk. "You will be paid when all the others are paid and not before."

"And when will that be?" Jodell asked.

"How should I know?" the commander snapped at him. "As soon as my clerks can finish tallying the damages."

"That could take weeks," Jodell said.

"Yes it could, perhaps even months," the commander said with a self-satisfied grin. Jodell stepped a little closer to the desk, rubbing on the scrub of beard that was starting to grow on his face.

"I see," Jodell said as he drew himself up to his full height. "Let me put it to you this way, little man." Jodell then opened his cloak and threw it back over his shoulder, exposing his sword and another dagger he kept in his belt.

"Now I am only going to say this once and I hope you get it right the first time." He put his hand on the pommel of his sword and drew it out just a little. "Either I leave here with my money in the next ten minutes or I leave here with your head. Either one will do. I do not care which. It is up to you."

The commander's hands had started to shake as his eyes moved from Jodell's eyes to his sword. "My guards are just outside. They could be here in a second."

"All I will require is half a second to remove your head," was Jodell's response.

"You would never get away from here alive." The commander was visibly shaking now. Jodell simply shrugged his shoulders and drew his sword out some more. At that moment, one of the guards stuck his head through the curtain.

"Commander, the king is here." Jodell allowed his sword to slide back into place and allowed a smile to form on his face. "It looks like you may get to keep your head a little longer, Sergeant," he said and he turned his attention to the tent entrance. The entrance curtains parted at that moment and the king entered.

"What was that about someone keeping his head?" the king asked as he moved around behind the desk.

"Oh, nothing, your highness. Your sergeant here was just deciding how much his head was worth in gold." The king looked at the commander who immediately dropped to one knee.

"Commander, what the hell is going on here?" The commander stood up but did not take his eyes from the floor.

"Your majesty he is demanding that he be paid. But . . ."

"Pay him then." The king cut him off.

"But, majesty, we have not finished . . ." The commander started but was again cut off by the king.

"Do you wish to argue with me, commander?"

"Of course not your majesty, it is just that we have not finished our tallies yet." The king sat down in the big chair behind the desk and sighed heavily.

"It's alright, commander, please pay him and be done with it."

"At once, your majesty." The commander drew himself up straight and threw a hastily formed salute. He glared at Jodell for a moment and then left the tent barking orders at the guards outside. The king then turned his attention back to Jodell who had been standing quietly with his arms folded across his chest.

"Was there something else you required?" The king's voice was matter of fact and cold. It was well known that he did not like mercenaries. However, Jodell did not care if he liked him or not as long as he paid him.

"There is another lying dead just outside the surgeon's tent. He was a friend of mine; a mercenary, like me. He asked that I give his pay to his wife and child. I said I would."

"So," was the king's response.

"He had not yet collected it. The law clearly states that a mercenary is always to be paid regardless of his affiliation with the winning or losing side."

"I know the law, mercenary." The king spat out the title as if it was acid on his tongue. "How much was he due?"

"Six hundred in gold," Jodell said matter of factly.

"That is an awful lot," the king said.

"I did not set the figure," Jodell said in reply. "Will you pay?"

"I will send the money to your tent within the hour."

"Very well," Jodell said then left the tent.

Jodell had planned to leave the camp by first light, before the rusty hue of the sun crested the horizon to the east. When the red-faced commander showed up at his tent with the money his plans changed quickly. "The king commands that you be given safe escort out of the province to say as far as the upland meadows of the land holdings of the old baron." Jodell took the gold and put it in his saddle bags without counting it.

"You may tell your king that it will not be necessary, I know the way, although I appreciate the thought." He had stopped his packing to look at the little man to emphasize his point. He already knew, however, that it was a mute point and would do him no good to argue. He resumed his packing, turning his back on the commander. He had hoped to get a good night's sleep before moving on in the morning.

"I am afraid," the commander continued," that I must insist on escorting you." Jodell could clearly read the pleasure in his voice. He turned and looked at the commander taking a step toward him. The commander nearly fell backward getting out of his way. Jodell moved around him and grabbed some more of his gear.

"I will be ready at the end of an hour if that is satisfactory to you." The commander had regained his composure as well as his courage when two of his guards had joined him.

"My orders are to escort you from the camp now," the commander said a little louder than was necessary. Jodell drew in a deep breath and let it out in a long sigh. He stopped his packing and spoke to the commander.

"Look, I want to be out of here just as badly as you want me out of here. But I can hardly pack with you and these two goons standing in my way. So why don't you all go away and come back later and we can talk some more then."

"Listen you flea bitten Sartorian son of a . . ." The commander stopped in mid-sentence. Jodell had drawn his sword and had it pinned against the commander's throat before the two guards even cleared their scabbards.

"You know, Sergeant," Jodell intoned, "You are really starting to try my patience. Now I told you to go away and come back in an hour and I meant that. Now we have a choice here. You can walk out on your own or we can have these two clowns each carry half of you out. Either way would suit me just fine but I will leave it up to you. What will it be?" When he moved his sword the commander hurried out of his tent without another word.

Jodell left the camp before the commander returned. He knew it was not above the man to have an arrow put in his back. He was tired of fighting, had had enough for one day.

Though he had to admit that he would very much have liked to relieve the commander of his fat head.

Jodell soon forgot about the commander. He made his way to the old monastery and fulfilled his promise to Karle. When he left the monastery it was well after midnight. He was traveling north by way of the main highway. It would take him first through the border cities of Karta and Memla then on through the heartland of Meriddia and the northern bluff forest. He had picked up the trail again and it led north. It was something he could sense in his marrow. Something that pulled at him and led his search.

A stranger had come to his home one day during a summer storm seeking shelter from the rain. He has welcomed him, taken him in. He still blamed himself for being too trusting and foolish, for when he woke the next morning the stranger had gone and taken his little girl with him. That had been nearly five years ago but still he searched for him. Rationally he knew he would never see his daughter again but he felt in his heart that he would one day find that man.

Jodell entered Drachna, a medium-sized city on the northern edge of Sartoe six weeks later.

Beneath a Dark Moon

One

The scent of roasted venison drifted upward in a cloud of black smoke mixing with the dark clouds that were gathering. Jodell sat at the edge of his fire, hunched against the chill night air, caressing a mug of hot spiced wine. He sat staring into the flames, his eyes watering from the heavy smoke, his face stinging from the cold. He sat unmoving, immersed in his thoughts, dreaming of when he was home with Jaecai, his beautiful little daughter. We could still see her small round face aglow with life, running through their small garden with tears of joy streaming down her face because her father was returning from the fields.

He remembered how he would sweep her up into his arms, how she would kiss him while rattling on about what she had done that day. She would lead him into the house, seat him at the table and serve his dinner, dinner she cooked herself especially for him.

How happy they had been together. She had been the joy of his life ever since her mother died. She was the only reason that kept him going; what he lived for. He reached into his belt pouch and pulled out a violet. A tear fell from his eyes as he turned it over in his fingers. It had been her favorite flower. She would tend them herself in a small sector of the garden. Every day she would pick one and give it to him, saying:

This is a symbol of our undying love, father.
I love you more than anything in the world.

He remembered one day how a stranger came to his home during a summer storm seeking shelter from the rain, how he foolishly took him in, and how he woke the next day to find the stranger and his daughter gone. That had been five years ago, he had been searching for her ever since. He had lived the life of a wanderer, hiring himself out as a mercenary or guard for living expenses. He had become well known in the Seven Kingdoms of Man and established a reputation as a fearless warrior and had been given the name Imack, which meant "death stare," by Lord Gountee, the king of the elves. Jodell sat with one hand over his mouth and the other gripping the flower, tears streaming down his cheeks.

Jodell lay down and wrapped himself in his blankets, his eyes still staring at the flames as they flickered and danced to some secret tune played by the gods, a slow and sensuous dance of loneliness and death. He felt his throat constrict and his chest tighten as water swelled in his eyes. He brought the violet up to his lips, his face contorting as he cried.

The sun shone with the brilliance of a million tapers lumped together behind Jodell's eyelids. His head hurt furiously, pain stabbing at the back of his eyes. The pain threatened to blind him if he kept his eyes closed, the sun threatening to blind him if he opened them. Jodell sat up slowly, his mind and body moving in degrees. He sat on his haunches, his face buried in his hands, rubbing at the pain and sleep in his eyes.

His thoughts still churned with the half hazy remnants of a nightmare that plucked at the fingers of his mind. Threatening to explode into his consciousness, but somehow stopped just short of breaching his defenses. He had long ago learned to contain his dreams just as he contained his fear in battle. His will was strong just like his body. He could abide almost anything. In fact, there had not been a single thing he had come up against that he had not faced head on and conquered except his memories.

His memories of Jaecai would return to him in his few moments of weakness and drag him down into a whirlpool of despair. His little girl had been stolen from him and he was left an empty shell, a hollow soulless man with no emotions, devoid of all sense of morality. The theft of his little girl had been the universal wrong, and beside that no other act could compare.

The morning air was chilly, and Jodell found himself shivering. He awoke in a pool of perspiration; his undergarments were wet with it. The chilly air stiffened his hide jerkins and jacket sending waves of cold through him. Jodell stood and stretched, welcoming the cold against his skin. It seemed to clear his head, driving away the ghosts from his mind.

His fire had died down to a flicker of wind-tossed embers that glowed in the morning breeze. Jodell quickly put it out, packed his gear and set out on the road again.

How long he rode was indeterminable. His quest had been a long one; he had come to appreciate his life. Indeed he felt safer, more relaxed under the stars than under a roof. Time dragged at an agonizingly slow pace for Jodell. His search had been long and arduous and he had learned patience.

His long journey through most of the seven kingdoms was spent in the saddle. He'd ridden through the torrential rains of the southern kingdoms, through the tricky marsh country of Aldmere. He had journeyed through the cold dreary northern kingdoms of Sartoe and Baldlordia, even venturing as far north as the icy wastelands of the Troll kingdoms. Here, the nights were long and the winds blew with the fury of the demigod Hecta.

The day quickly turned to evening. The sun was still up over the horizon, though fast condensing into a yellow orange mass that told of nightfall nearing. Jodell sat in his saddle, insensitive to his surroundings. The wind had picked up, screeching through the upper branches of the tall oaks that comprised most of the forest canopy. A few dead leaves were tossed into Jodell's face as he wound his way through the forest. He kept mostly to the road, sometimes veering off through the trees to avoid a dead tree that had fallen across it. The road was thickly covered with a mulch of dead leaves and rotting branches. Wild blackberries grew at its edges dropping overripe berries onto the road like blue-black bird droppings tracing a trail into the distance.

A few branches stretched out across the road, long thick branches flexing in the wind like giant digits grabbing for anyone passing. Through it all Jodell rode—his eyes fixed on pseudo bird droppings, his mind fixed on Jaecai.

The sounds of day finally gave in to the cry of night as the night stalkers came out to peruse the land. The moon was full tonight, its face glowing shyly down on earth below its iridescent feet, spreading long dull white arms across the black horizon, hugging the land like an alabaster mother with a Nubian child. She dreamily looking down on her night child. The child crying out in the darkness reaching for its mother with love-starved fingers. She responding with soft milk-white light, bringing comfort to the land.

Jodell made his camp for the night. He sat atop a small boulder, his face elevated toward the moon, drinking her milk, letting it soak into his body as his mind drifted with the winds.

Two

The streets were filled with merchants selling their wares from stalls. There were spices from Aldmere. Perfumes and fragrant oils from the middle kingdoms of Mereddia and Tithe. There were silks from the East and fine wines from the North. All were gathered together into one big moving mass. Jodell made his way down the small side streets, pushing his way through the throngs of people.

People were stopped in the street to watch a juggler toss glass balls into the air or a tumbler dazzle them with his feats. On one corner there was a magician, on another corner a bard. Every sort of person was on the street peddling their trade. Soldiers in light summer mail dotted the streets here and there watching over the crowd, keeping order. The air was heavy with the odors of food and perspiration mixed with the smell of manure—human and animal.

On one corner a huge man stood eating pies; a crowd gathered around him, urging him on. Jodell was reminded he had not had his breakfast and soon found his way to an inn.

The inn wasn't crowded, much to Jodell's relief. He seated himself at a table near the back wall in a shadowed corner. The innkeeper brought a huge mug of cold ale and set it on the table and stood staring down at Jodell.

Jodell didn't move at first but spoke in a toneless voice as he raised the mug to his lips. "Bring me something to eat," he said.

"What will you have?" the innkeeper's voice had a rough crackly sound that grated on Jodell's nerves, sending a shudder through him. Jodell took another drink from his mug. The ale was the best he had tasted in many months. It warmed his stomach, effectively fighting back his gnawing hunger. He raised his head and stared into the innkeeper's eyes, his light grey eyes piercing.

The innkeeper stared back for a few seconds and finally dropped his head. He was visibly shaken as he began rubbing his fat red hands together, his eyes searching the floor. When next he spoke his tone was softer and his voice lowered.

"All I have left is some hot stew," he continued looking at the wine stained floor, unable or unwilling to meet Jodell's eyes again.

"That will be fine," Jodell responded.

Jodell finished his dinner and sat sipping on a cup of wine, his mind wandering as it traced over the last few years of his life. He felt empty, his life unfulfilled and would remain so until he found his daughter.

Jodell felt tears begin to swell in his eyes and forced them back. The innkeeper had been standing at the other end of the room talking to another man who had recently arrived, both of them looking back at Jodell periodically.

"Who is he, Eric?" the other man spoke softly to the innkeeper. His eyes cutting across the room at Jodell.

"Don't know, never seen him before. Must be a stranger come to town for the festival." The innkeeper leaned on the bar, his massive head resting on fat red knuckles, his small rat-like eyes darting between Jodell and his friend.

"Don't look like folk from around here though. Look how he's dressed, he must have travelled from some distance. Those ain't no peasant's clothes," said the innkeeper.

"Yeah I know. Did you get a look at his sword? That's an expensive piece. The pommel must be pure gold. I gotta have that sword." The other man got off his stool and started toward Jodell. The innkeeper grabbed his arm his eyes darting around nervously.

"Knub, don't start any trouble in here. I don't want the soldiers coming in here." Knub turned, glancing down at the hand restraining him. The innkeeper felt the cold stare on his hand, his skin crawled. Knub was well known as a person with a hot temper and quick to draw his sword. He was also the best swordsman in town. Knub put his hand on his sword rubbing it affectionately. He was aware of his reputation and relished the respect it afforded him. He seldom missed an opportunity to reinforce his reputation. He looked up at the innkeeper, a cynical smile forming on his face.

"Eric! Eric! You worry too much." He grabbed the right side of Eric's face, pinching a handful of cheek, causing Eric to wince in pain.

"I'm only going to get to know him." Knub gave a wry smile as he walked away. Eric stood looking after him, rubbing his reddened cheek.

"Excuse me, my friend, may I join you?" Knub stood on the other side of the table facing Jodell, one hand on his sword hilt and the other leaning on the table. Jodell didn't look up, he'd already seen the man approaching him. He kept his eyes on Knub's sword hand, while gesturing for him to be seated and continuing to sip his wine. Knub sipped on his own wine for a moment then finally spoke.

"The wine here is the best in the territory. It's made right here you know. Eric, that's our innkeeper, makes it himself." Jodell continued staring into his mug.

"What's your name, friend? You're new around here aren't you? Do you know someone here in town. What's your business here?"

Jodell still did not answer. He simply slowly lifted his head to look at Knub. His long thick black hair hung unkempt onto his shoulders, framing his face, adding to the already deep shadows under his eyes. His clear grey eyes focused on Knub's and held them. Knub tried to return the stare, but soon faltered and looked away. He had never found anyone who could match his stare until now. This unnerved him. His hand instinctively moved toward his sword. Jodell didn't move, his expression didn't change. He sat with his eyes fixed on Knub. Knub caught himself and put both hands back on the table. He leaned back in his chair with a sigh, a wry smile forming on his lips.

"My, my, aren't we a strange one." He tried to sound hard when he spoke, but a slight hint of uneasiness slipped through.

"Look, friend," Knub said. "If I bother you just say so and I'll leave you alone. But I figure you're a stranger here and from the looks of you, you've come pretty far. Few people venture this far north this time of year, so I figure you must be looking for something or someone. That is where I can help. I know everyone and everything that goes on within one hundred miles of here. But then you don't look interested so I'll leave you." Knub went to get up and leave. Jodell spoke then but very softly. He was still staring at Knub.

"Go on," he said.

"Well, you do talk," Knub said.

"You were saying," Jodell responded.

"I can help you. My name is Knub." He extended his hand. Jodell looked from Knub's eyes to his hand then back to his eyes, his expression never changing. Knub closed his hand as he sat back down, his expression changing to one of apprehension. He had never met anyone who acted so strange, so solemn. He was known in this town for his disposition. This stranger that unnerved even him was a threat. His curiosity was pricked, he had to find out who this man was and what he wanted.

Jodell finished his wine and gestured to the innkeeper for a refill. He fixed his eyes on Knub again this time without the cold hard stare yet still retaining an air of detached impersonal resentment. He studied Knub's deep recessed hairline. Knub's face was structured, his features very prominent. His cheek bones were his most prominent feature. They sat on the sides of his face like small red mountains. Unlike most of the men from the North, he wore no beard, only a light mustache. His face was very thin and gave the impression of a man spindly built. His eyes, however, overshadowed any fault of feature that he may have had. His eyes were huge pit black balls that darted from side to side. He was somewhat of an anomaly. His eyes contrasted vividly with his near white hair.

"Why would you want to help me?" Jodell asked.

Knub smiled. "You look like a good sort, and, well that's just my nature. You know, help your fellow man and all that." Knub sat back in his chair smiling at Jodell. "You could say I'm a humanitarian. Yeah, that's it, I'm a humanitarian."

Jodell sat straight in his chair, his expression unchanged. "Perhaps you can help me at that. I'm looking for someone. A man, tall, black hair with deep-set black eyes, like yours." Jodell's expression changed at that. He could see him in his mind. He would never forget his face. A long thin face as pale as goat's milk. Deep-set black eyes that blazed with a dark fire. That long thin nose that came to a needle point. He would never forget that face.

"I've been tracking him and his trail leads here." Knub sat forward in his chair, thinking, rubbing his chin.

"Doesn't sound familiar. Don't think I've seen this guy around here." Knub stopped and thought for a few seconds, then shook his head. "No, haven't seen him. I tell you what I can do. I'll ask around and if this man you're looking for is here, in town, I'll find out."

Knub finished his wine in one gulp. "There is one small detail we have overlooked. There is a matter of payment."

"How much?" Jodell intoned. Knub smiled and licked his lips.

"Enough to buy a sword like yours."

"If you find him the sword will be yours." Knub sat back, a smile of satisfaction on his face. He drained his second cup of wine, sighing aloud as he finished it.

Jodell had returned to looking into his cup, his mind occupied with his wandering thoughts, his emotion-racked memories. Knub leaned forward putting both hands on the table and spoke.

"Why are you looking for this guy? If I knew, it might help me to locate him." Jodell slowly raised his head to look at Knub, then slowly stood.

"I am staying here at the inn, if you find out anything, this is where I will be." Jodell reached into his pocket and pulled out a gold coin and put it on the table.

"This wine is on me." He walked away, secured a room for the night, then disappeared upstairs. Knub and Eric looked after him, Eric in awe, Knub with bitter disdain.

Jodell's room was a small cubicle outfitted with a small bed and a nightstand which stood at the head. There was a bronze pitcher of water and a small matching bowl beside it for washing. Jodell stood in the doorway a few seconds, eyeing his room. He went over to the nightstand, poured some water into the bowl, stared down at the reflections of an old man in the water, his grey speckled hair falling to his shoulders. He starred at the reflection of the stranger with the sad eyes that looked back at him. He allowed a half-smile, half-frown to form on one side of his face. It had been a long time since he had really taken a good look at himself. He ran his hand through his hair; craned his neck until it popped.

Jodell sat on the edge of the bed, a sudden surge of fatigue coming over him. He lay back and closed his eyes. It had been awhile since he last slept in a bed, he had nearly forgotten how comfortable they were. It would not have mattered, however, whether he was in bed or lying on the hard ground. He was exhausted. His body ached with it. His eyes were a glazed fiery red behind his lids. He lay back with his hand across his forehead, his mind racing. He wanted to get up and wash but was too tired. Darkness slowly crept in as he gave in to his exhaustion. Sleep was quick in coming.

*   *   *

The tavern was a small cluster of rooms whose walls had been torn down to make a moderate-sized hall. It was a dark place filled with the pungent odors of stale wine, urine, perspiration, vomit and smoke from the peat lamps that burned in the corners. It was a rather foreboding place of shadows and filth.

The floors were caked with sticky wine and molded food. Drunks could be seen standing in corners relieving their ale and rum filled bladders, or their overtaxed stomachs.

The tavern had been built with double doors to keep out the cold, which also very effectively kept all fresh air out and stale air in. Thus, the tavern got its name, "THE HOUSE OF FUMES." Knub and a few of his men sat at a back table huddled close together in conversation. Knub spoke rather softly, his words meant only for the ears of his men.

"This guy says he's looking for someone. I told him we would help him." Knub sipped his wine as he spoke, his fingers running up and down the hilt of his sword.

"Okay, you all know what to do. Scar, you and Gregor hide out back and wait for my signal. Don't come out until you hear me cough; twice. Dan, you wait in here. I'll go get

11

him and bring him here. I'll take him out through the back where Scar and Gregor will be waiting. You follow us out, but stay out of sight until you hear my signal."

Everyone nodded in agreement as Knub's dark eyes fell upon each one of them in turn.

*   *   *

It was dark when Jodell awakened the next day. His sleep-drenched mind unable to orient itself. He lay back with his eyes open, staring into the darkness of his room. Again, he fought with his memories. His stomach flipped as a vision of Jaecai came to him, smiling shyly at him, her love for him showing in her eyes. Jodell shut his eyes on his vision as tears streamed down his face, wetting his pillow.

How many times had he seen her face? How many times had he cried out in anguish, prayed in despair? How many faces had he seen that reminded him of her, bringing back those torturous memories? How long had he searched for her and her abductor?

For the first time in five years he was close. He could feel it. There was something in the air, a fleeting scent, a faint sensation, an aura that plucked at the periphery of his mind. He was aware of something tangible in the air that stayed just out of reach. He knew he was close, closer than he had ever been before.

Somehow she was close to him, within his reach. "But where, where?" Jodell spoke aloud as the words formed in his mind. He was nearly lost in his world of despair. A world he sank deeper and deeper into as the years went by. At times he would go into his private world and stay there. There he could be happy. There he could be with his Jaecai, watching her run through the fields of their small farm, picking flowers—hair flying in the winds as she ran to him, her face aglow and full of life.

He would stay in his little world where he and Jaecai could be alone, where only the two of them mattered. In their world, everything existed for them and they existed for each other.

Jodell still lay back in his bed. A tear rolled from his eyes leaving a salty track across his face, ending in his right ear. A small peaceful smile had formed on his face, his eyes seeing another world, another time. He was with his daughter, oblivious to the world outside his room. The world outside could have died and he would not have known, neither would he have cared, because for the moment he was where he wanted to be. He was home.

*   *   *

Jodell and Knub emerged from the rear door of the tavern. It was completely dark except for a small amount of light that bounced off the dingy walls of the houses and found its way down the alley with a hazy blue-green hue. Jodell walked slowly beside Knub, his eyes searching the corners of the alley instinctively. The air was slightly damp, a low hanging fog was developing, leaving droplets of condensed water dripping from the end of his hair, running down his neck, chest and back in small rivers. The water was cool as it ran across his body sending little shivers through him, refreshing him.

Knub had not spoken a word since they emerged from the tavern. He looked about nervously, his eyes darting across the alley. He brought his right hand up to his mouth to cough and at the same time, slowly reached across for his sword.

Jodell's eye caught the faint glimmer of light that bounced off Dan's sword blade from one corner of the alley. He calculated the distance between him and Dan and readied himself. Knub was slowly inching away from him. Knub he could see and thus deal with. He was more concerned at this point with the sounds behind him.

13

Knub coughed twice and darted into the shadows. Gregor and Scar came out of hiding and approached Jodell slowly from opposite sides. Scar's sword was poised, the tip elevated, pointing at Jodell's throat. Dan approached him from behind. Gregor and Scar approached together. Scar would wait for Jodell to engage Gregor, and while he was defending himself from attack from both front and back, he would move in for the kill. Scar approached Jodell smiling, his heavy features radiating pleasure at the upcoming kill.

Jodell stood perfectly still, his right hand reached across to his sword hilt, his left hand holding his dagger by the blade. He waited. There was silence for a few tense moments. The wind had picked up, slightly blowing his hair about his face. The air was brisk yet pleasant and Jodell relaxed as he waited for his time to strike.

Suddenly Dan screamed and charged, Gregor followed suit and moved in. Jodell spun and threw his dagger side armed; the blade landed in the sink of Dan's neck. He stopped in his tracks, blood gurgling from his mouth, his eyes opened wide with astonishment as he sank to his knees and toppled over. Jodell's momentum carried him full circle. As he came around, he whipped out his sword, bringing it up and across from left to right, keeping his head low. Gregor's sword swooshed over his head. Jodell's sword entered Gregor's stomach and cut upward, the force of the blow cutting through Gregor's ribs, severing his heart and emerging through his left shoulder. He was dead before he hit the ground.

Scar stood facing Jodell, his sword in hand, his eyes darting from Jodell to the lifeless forms of his two companions. Knub stood off to one side, his eyes squinted against the shadows. Scar was visibly shaken by the speed at which Jodell had dispatched his friends. Jodell stood with his legs spread in a defensive stance, his sword hanging down by his side. Blood ran from the tip of his sword, dripping in a larger pool that was forming about his feet. Jodell stared at Scar, fixing him with his stare. Scar stared back, a flicker of recognition flashing across his face.

"Imack," Scar whispered the name to himself. Knub heard him but not clearly.

"Knub, do you know who we have here? This is the famous Imack." Knub squinted his eyes even more in a vain attempt to see clearly.

"Are you sure? There's no mistake?" Scar took a small step forward. Jodell's sword immediately whipped up, the entire movement coming from the wrist, his body's position didn't change.

Scar smiled a wry complacent smile, cocking his head back to one side. "Oh, I'm sure. We've met before, under similar circumstances. Yes, I'm sure alright, I'd know that sword technique anywhere." Scar's smile faded as he ran his finger along the line of a scar that started at his right hip and ran the length of his stomach and chest, crossing from right to left.

Scar circled to his left, placing himself between Knub and Jodell, "Stay out of this. He's mine. We have a score to settle!"

Scar moved in to attack, Jodell met him. Their swords clashed again and again, sparks flew, neither man gave way to the other. They circled each other, each one looking for weak spots in the other's defenses. Scar attacked again. Jodell met the blow with his sword, stepping inside at the same time. He delivered a knee to Scar's stomach. Scar winced in pain. Jodell took advantage. He slid his sword down Scar's blade in a short downward slice. He severed the thumb from the left hand and sliced the back of the right hand to the bone.

Scar howled in pain as he dropped his sword and fell to his knee's, blood gushing from both hands. He held his hands out in front of him and elevated his head to look at Jodell. Jodell brought his sword down again and severed both hands at the wrist. Scar screamed and fell forward, sprawled in his own blood, which ran in small thick streams slowly mixing with the already congealed blood of this two companions. Jodell watched him for a few seconds, then brought his sword down in a circular arc, severing Scar's head from his body. He then turned his attention to Knub, who was still standing in awe.

*   *   *

Jodell made his way back to the inn. He dragged along as if a heavy chain was attached to his legs, dragging a dead weight. He walked stolidly, a tall petulant anachronism, standing stark against the blue-black heavens.

The darkness heaved against his neck, crawled and curled around his neck until he thought he would choke. He stopped in the middle of the street, his mind raced with a million thoughts, a million anguished questions, all irrevocably tied to his quest for his daughter. He brought his hand up to his face, wiped a tear from his eyes.

He held his hand to his cheek, stifling a sob that rose in his chest. After a few minutes, he realized he had stopped and was standing in the middle of the street. He took a step forward, his knees felt weak; about to buckle. He stopped again trying to gain control of himself, trying to master his anguish. He took another step, then another. His head swooned, the night seemed to crawl up his body and blacken his vision. He strained to open his eyes and see what was ahead of him. All he could see was his past.

Jodell felt himself slipping, falling as if he had been hanging by a cord over a great pit until it snapped and he fell. He reached out in all directions, grasping for something to hold onto, something or someone. He cried out to himself. His cries floated on the cool night air that rushed past him, whipping through his thrashing fingers as he fell. He cried until his eyes ached and his voice died and all he could do was fall, unable to stop himself.

Then there was nothing, no sounds, no sensations, only darkness, thick darkness that encapsulated his mind, imprisoning him in a world of despair.

Jodell collapsed to the ground, his chest heaving as he struggled to contain his emotions. He sat on his knees, his chin against his chest, his eyes closed against the tears that rose behind his lids. After a few long moments, he opened his eyes. At first he didn't recognize his surroundings. He felt a strange yet familiar sensation start to rise in the pit of his stomach. He recognized it but refused to acknowledge it. Refused to accept it. But he was in the end, too weak to withstand it.

Fear settled around his heart, and plucked at his being, until his hackles rose like a trapped animal, too afraid of death to stay and too afraid of life to run.

Jodell lifted his head, his eyes focusing slowly on the small yellow light that burned over the doorway of the inn. He stood slowly, his body swaying like a young tree being blown by the wind. He stood shakily on half numbed feet and shambled forward toward the inn. He found his way to the back stairs and up to his room. He unlocked the door and pushed his way in, collapsing on the bed. He lay on his stomach, his eyes scouring the darkness of his room, and found no light, no comfort for his aching soul. He wanted to cry again, but couldn't. There were no more tears. No more emotions to vent. He felt empty, desolate, alone and despised. Above all, he felt hated not so much by others than by himself. He had lost his wife, and now his daughter. He was unable to forgive himself. He lay in bed staring into the darkness oblivious to everything but the lead weight that lay in his chest.

Three

Jodell woke late the next evening to the throbbing of his own heart. He rolled over in bed, his face contorting at the pain that rushed from the back of his head and stabbed painfully at his closed eyelids. He lay on his back, a slight shiver traversing his body.

The day had started out nice but had chilled late. The sun disappeared behind heavy clouds and the day became cold and depressing. His door to his room was still open, swinging in the evening breeze, banging against the wall, adding to the already clamorous sounds that filled his head.

Jodell came around slowly, some of the haze that clouded his mind cleared, he was able to sit up on the edge of the bed. He bent forward, buried his head in his palms, pressed the heels of his hands into his eyes, rubbing at the small pebbles that seemed to tear at them. He stood, poured some water in the bowl on the nightstand, washed. The water was ice cold. He applied it to his face until his face felt numb. Slowly he was able to see as his mind cleared of the last vestiges of cobwebs that had so completely clouded his mind.

As Jodell wiped the water from his face, he stared at his reflection in the dirt and blood-colored water. It was the same one that he'd seen last night. He saw a stranger whose small eyes were drawn and puffy underneath with heavy wrinkles forming at the corners. Deep lines were etched into the forehead and the corners of the mouth seemed to turn down in a perpetual snarl.

His reflection stared back at him with cold, hazy grey eyes. There was no joy in those eyes, only pain and hatred. He brought his hand up to his face, his rough prickly beard scratched the back of his hand as he wiped it across his mouth in a vain attempt to erase some of the pain.

It was nearly dark when he finished washing. He paid his bill and had a light meal before leaving the inn. He collected his horse and left, forever moving north.

*   *   *

The sun soon settled over the northern range of the Ca-vryll Mountains and a full moon appeared to take its place. The north was really a small cramped trail that wound its way through the forest. Here the vegetation was thick and overgrown. The road was seldom used. Any people entering the town usually came from the South. This road was mainly used as a trail into the forest by the townspeople for hunting or foraging for wild vegetables and nuts.

It was late in the night when Jodell finally stopped to rest, sometime around midnight. The forest was nearly pitch black. He had become accustomed to the darkness after spending so much time on the road. He was able to see well enough by the thin moonlight to make out the winding of the road.

The night air was still cold. Jodell sat before his fire, a small pot of mulled ale steamed over it as he sipped at a small cup of it. The ale warned him and soon he found himself dozing.

Jodell woke with a shiver. His fire had died down to a low flicker and the night air had become a little cooler. He stirred the fire and added a few more twigs, got the fire blazing again and poured himself another cup of ale.

It was past midnight, the moon was still shining brightly, casting long shadows across the clearing where he camped.

19

Jodell brought his cup up to his lips to take a sip, he hesitated, listening. Something was wrong. The insects had stopped chattering. He took another sip, listening. There was the sound of stealthily approaching footsteps, just barely audible. Jodell slowly reached for his dagger that was strapped to his left leg. Slowly he withdrew it from its sheath. He held it by the blade and waited. Waiting for the footsteps to get a little closer. By now he could feel the presence of someone at his back. He hunched his back getting ready. He spoke softly to himself.

"Steady now, steady. Not yet, not yet . . . just a little closer." A twig snapped. "Now!"

Jodell spun and dived to the side at the same time throwing his dagger side armed behind him. He was rather tall, a little taller than Jodell but thin, yet not scrawny. His hair was long and silver grey and hung down in back, tied neatly together by a silver clasp, that was a coiled snake. The front of his robe had a snake embroidered into it with silver thread and was tied together in front by a silver braided cord that hung nearly to his feet. His eyes were a deep sapphire blue that seemed to sparkle slightly as they picked up some of the light from Jodell's fire. He stood at the periphery of Jodell's camp. He was carrying a long staff which was ebony and terminated in a silver serpent's head, mouth opened, fangs bared. He carried a traveling sack across his back. He stood with Jodell's dagger in his hand, turning it over and over admiring it.

"A beautiful weapon you have here, very well balanced." Jodell stood up straight but didn't remove his eyes from his visitor nor did he lower his sword.

"Who are you?" Jodell asked, his tone neutral.

"My name is Katrill," the old man answered.

"Who are you?" Jodell raised his voice slightly. The old man stepped forward as he started to speak again. Jodell arched his sword from left to right.

"Hold!" Jodell's voice was threatening. "I will not hesitate to kill you, old man. Now, drop my dagger." Katrill dropped the dagger in front of himself and then spoke.

"I don't want any trouble. On the contrary, I only wish to share your fire and your company. Travelling is a lonely occupation, and the night is cold." Jodell said nothing, he simply stood watching Katrill. After a few moments Katrill spoke again.

"I come in peace and do not want any trouble, however, if you prefer it, I will turn and leave you to your solitude." He watched Jodell for a few seconds. Jodell neither spoke nor moved. Katrill smiled slightly then turned to leave.

"Old man." Katrill stopped and turned. Jodell resheathed his sword and gestured for Katrill to be seated. He went to the fire, poured himself and Katrill a cup of ale.

"I am deeply in your debt. Your kindness shall be rewarded in kind." Jodell sat quietly sipping his ale. He watched Katrill over the rim of his cup through the vapors. Katrill drained his cup and sighed deeply with pleasure. He gestured toward the pot of ale, a crank smile on his face.

"May I? It has been a long time since I've had a good hot cup of ale." Jodell bowed his consent.

For a long time the two sat before the fire, across from each other, neither speaking. The night air grew a little cooler as the night breeze picked up a little, blowing leaves about in little swirls, creating minute dust devils.

It was well past midnight, Jodell was tired but was unable to sleep. He added some kindling to his fire and prepared a small meal of stewed potatoes and venison. He shared his meal with his visitor. He himself ate very little.

Jodell raised his head and looked up at the stars. The North Star blazed in the sky, seemingly directly above him, like a beacon that promised to lead him to another land where he and his little girl would be together again. Jodell closed his eyes on his vision, squeezing his lids tight, forcing back a tear.

It was at these times that he was his weakest, his most vulnerable. At these times when he sat out under the stars, when the wind blew a gentle breeze across his face and tossed a lock of silvered black hair against his chest. It was at these times that his emotions rose in his chest and threatened to swell in his eyes like a river ready to crest after a heavy rain.

Jodell plucked a wild flower that was growing beside him. He traced the intricacies of its petals with his fingers. A lone tear perched itself in the corner of one eye and slowly rolled down his cheek, falling into the center of the flower. Katrill watched him for a moment, then spread his blanket on the ground before the fire and lay down, turning his back to the flames and Jodell, leaving him with his grief.

*   *   *

The morning was vibrant and alive. The air was still chilly though not so much as the night before. The forest was alive with activity. Jodell was already stirring when Katrill woke. He had rebuilt the fire and had already prepared a small breakfast. He was packing his blankets onto his saddle. Katrill stood slowly, stretching. His deep blue eyes were rimmed in red as he fought off the last vestiges of sleep.

"Good morning, my friend," Katrill spoke to Jodell as he poured himself a cup of hot ale and skeetered a small piece of bacon. Jodell responded slowly to this early morning greeting, just barely nodding his head in response.

"It promises, I think, to be a fine day. Yes, I think so. A fine day for traveling, don't you think?" Jodell walked across the clearing passing Katrill and spoke as he passed, his eyes on the ground in front of him.

"Yeah, a fine day for traveling." He moved to the other side of the fire across from Katrill and picked up his sword and vestment and strapped it on.

"Where are you headed?" Katrill asked.

"North." Jodell finished packing his horse, put out his fire and mounted. He was in no mood for conversation, his brain ached and he needed to be alone.

The days were getting shorter as they moved further north. The air was getting cooler and the forest thinning out.

Jodell rode solemnly all day not stopping for lunch. Katrill was following close. It was nearly dark when Jodell called a halt, allowing Katrill to catch up to him.

"Old man, why are you following me? You've been following me for days now. What do you want?" Jodell spoke in a dispassionate tone while his mist grey eyes transfixed Katrill.

"Ah, my friend, it is as you say. I have been following you. I had hoped to join you in search of your daughter." Jodell's face flushed red, his eyes blazed. He had not spoken to this man about his search. Jodell shifted his position in his saddle, leaned forward, and spoke slowly and softly.

"Who are you, old man?" Jodell asked.

"My name is Katrill, I told you that already."

"Do not tease me, old man," Jodell scowled at Katrill. "I'm not in the mood." Katrill lifted his head, drew a deep breath and smiled. When next he spoke, his voice was lower, sounding tired, older.

"Ah, my young friend, you are a hard one indeed. I was warned you would not be easy to assimilate." Katrill returned his attention to Jodell, smiling warmly. "Come, let us make camp, and I will tell you all you need to know," said Katrill.

"This is not a good place to camp; not enough shelter. We will camp over there." Jodell pointed to a small grove of spruce trees setting off to themselves as if they had been purposely planted.

Darkness finally came, wrapping itself around Jodell and Katrill, immersing them in a sea of blackness. The night air was damp and chilly and seemed to flow rather than blow. The moon was out and at its zenith. It glowed like a beacon, a haven of light in a pit of blackness promising shelter and warmth.

The sky itself was a black monolith, a huge dark entity that tried to pass itself off as an angel of light. It competed with the land for the moon's light, sucking it up until there was none left for the light-starved land. Yet, it offered its own light, small, brightly twinkling patches of bluish-white light that affected the souls of those who, in their weaker moments, turned to it for consolation.

"It's beautiful, isn't it?" Katrill sat with his back to a tree, his staff leaning across his lap, the silver serpentine head reflecting the deep hues of the camp fire.

Jodell turned his head slowly, blinking the stars out of his eyes. "What is?"

"The night sky," Katrill replied softly, as he continued to scan the night sky. "It is a thing of beauty and power, a power often misused."

"What do you mean?" Jodell asked.

"I'm afraid I don't really know. It is beyond my meager abilities to comprehend." Jodell turned his head away from Katrill and watched the fire.

"You talk in riddles, old man."

"Life is a riddle, my young friend. The answers to all your questions are a product of that riddle. One riddle leads to another and another. The more answers you have, the more riddles you must answer. The more riddles you solve, the more questions you have that need to be answered. The wise man accepts what life offers without questions."

Jodell stood and paced before the fire. "I cannot accept what life has offered me. It has given me nothing but grief and anguish and that, no man should have to accept."

"What you say is true," Katrill responded, "no man should. In truth most men do not, and that is where the problem lies. It is in the nature of man to question everything he does not understand and change everything he does. In the end he creates more problems for himself than he started with."

"You still speak in riddles, old man. You have not answered my question." Katrill poured himself another cup of wine and drained it, pouring himself another.

"I will give you all the answers you desire that are in my power to give in due course. But first, you have a lesson to learn and that will, in the end, answer many questions."

"And what is that?" Jodell asked.

Katrill leaned back against his tree, staring up at Jodell, his light blue eyes dancing in the fire light.

"My friend, do not be so hasty to learn too much at once. You are like a child, one teaches them slowly. If you teach them too much too fast, you lose them. Be patient my young friend, be patient."

Jodell stood and watched Katrill for a few moments then walked over to the other side of his campfire. He laid out his sleeping blanket and lay down.

It wasn't long before Katrill was asleep, his heavy labored breathing mostly drowned out by the crackling of the fire. The night air remained cool but still. Jodell lay on his back, he could not sleep. His mind was restless. He lay back thinking about all the things that Katrill had said to him, but none of it seemed to make any sense. The only thing Jodell knew for sure was that Katrill wasn't going to tell him anything.

Jodell fell into a half-sleep. His body tired, his mind tired, but his spirit was restless, his dreams haunting him again. Dreams of his daughter came to him. He could see her face, her long black hair swinging as she ran toward him, arms outstretched to hug him, then she disappeared. He called her name over and over, trying to find her but she did not answer. He ran in all directions calling her. Then he saw her lying across a boulder on her stomach, arms outstretched to either side. Her eyes closed and her chest still.

Jodell stood back and watched her. He wanted to go to her but was too afraid of what he would find. She began to move, sat up and stared at him, smiling. Jodell watched her, his heart pounding. She came toward him. At first, he could not see her face clearly, only her features were visible. He wanted to run to her and run away at the same time. Somehow she was his daughter, yet, he felt that at the same time she was not. His feet would not move. He shut his eyes and waited until he felt a small hand on his. It was a cold touch that made his skin crawl. He opened his eyes and screamed.

Katrill stood over him trying to wake him. Jodell sat up suddenly, grabbing Katrill's shirt. He pulled him toward him. He was still breathing heavily.

"Did you see her? Did you see her?"

"See whom?" Katrill asked.

"Did you see . . ." Jodel stopped himself. He released Katrill, dropping his hands by his side. He closed his eyes and sighed heavily. "I'm sorry, I'm fine now."

"Are you sure, you were having a bad dream?" Katrill was still standing over Jodell, his eyes still glazed over by sleep.

"I'll be alright, go back to sleep." Jodell stood and walked to the edge of the camp, peering into the thick darkness that hovered just beyond the reach of his fire light.

"You should rest, my young friend," Katrill admonished.

"I can't, you go back to sleep. I'll be okay." Katrill still stood, looking at him. He walked over to Jodell placing his hand on his shoulder. Jodell turned, looking into his eyes.

Katrill spoke softly, "You will sleep, my young friend, and you will forget." His finger touched Jodell's forehead,

Jodell's eyes fluttered shut and he fell forward, asleep. Katrill caught him and placed him on his blanket.

Katrill sat up for the rest of the night. He made a fresh pot of hot wine and brought the fire back to a roar. Jodell slept peacefully, his breathing deep and restful.

The new morning found Jodell still asleep. Katrill dozed off near dawn. The birds began to come out and woke Katrill with their shrill songs. Katrill brought the fire back up and prepared a light breakfast of dehydrated potatoes and boiled pork.

After washing, he packed his horse and searched for the best possible path to follow north through the heavy bush, while Jodell slept. Jodell woke shortly before noon. The air had warmed considerably, but there was no sun. The day was a repeat of the day before, dreary, but slightly warmer.

Four

The land stretched out in waves like frozen ripples on a dead sea. The ground was hard and packed. Wild grass grew in intermittent patches, swaying in the afternoon wind. The ground looked baked and parched though the temperature seldom rose above sixty degrees. There were very few trees in this part of the North. Those that there were, were mostly small sturdy things with little foliage.

It was mid-August and already the signs of winter could be felt in the air. The sparse vegetation was already turning brown. The wind was beginning to pick up blowing loose surface dirt and leaves.

Jodell and Katrill hunched against the chill air and rode side by side in silence. Jodell was pensive as usual. Katrill let him be, allowing him his solitude. When Jodell finally spoke, it was in an empty monotone as if he were uninterested in what he himself was saying. His eyes, however, bespoke of a man very much aware.

"Old man, tell me what you know about the 'Hated One.'" Katrill's eyes flashed. He had not expected Jodell to be so blunt and in truth, had not expected Jodell to know the name.

"Where have you heard this name?" Katrill asked. His voice displayed no emotion though he shifted in his saddle nervously.

"I've heard it mentioned in certain circles or perhaps I should say, whispered." Jodell was scanning the distant horizon while talking.

"What else have you heard about this 'Hated One' as you have called him?" Katrill asked, probing to find how much Jodell already knew.

"Old man, you answer the question with a question." Katrill rubbed the head of his serpentine staff. It rested in a leather carrier on his right side. It gleamed in the dwindling sunlight, reflecting the deep orange of the setting sun.

"What is your interest in him?" Katrill asked.

"Damn it, old man, can't you for once answer a question without asking another?"

"You're right, I'm sorry. His name is Jebeialle, he is a member of my clan." Katrill's eyes glistened as he remembered his youth. "I was a young apprentice Thermarage when we first met. He was a Thermarage, second order. It was the tradition of the upper clansmen to befriend the new apprentices. He became my guide and later my friend."

The sun finally settled. The wind picked up and the air got cooler. Storm clouds were gathering in the eastern sky and moving westerly. Jodell knew that it would soon be raining heavily. He and Katrill would be caught in a storm without shelter.

It was nearly dark, the sky lightened intermittently by lightning. The sky was filled with dark storm clouds, thunder sounded in from the East like huge drum rolls. Jodell spotted a wisp of black smoke drifting upward and turned his horse in that direction.

Jodell and Katrill pulled up before a small cabin with a thatch roof. The cabin was small and dark, no lights were on and there was no sign of movement. Jodell sat on his horse and looked at the cabin. Katrill pulled up beside him and touched his arm.

"My friend, I do not like this place. There is something wrong." Jodell sat back in his saddle, took a deep breath and spoke without taking his eyes off the cabin.

29

"What is it?" Jodell asked.

"I cannot be sure. There is something unsettling about this cabin. Just something I feel, something I've felt before somewhere, but I can't remember where." Katrill brought his hand up to his face and rubbed back a few loose strands of silvered grey hair that had fallen across his eye.

"Be that as it may," Jodell said, "we shall have to stay here for the night. I don't want to be caught out in the storm that's brewing."

Jodell dismounted and walked his horse to the front door, tying it under the porch canopy. Katrill did the same.

"I don't think anyone is here. This house looks deserted. I don't think anyone has lived here for quite some time," Katrill said as he stood back and surveyed the cabin curiously.

The cabin was dark except for a faint red glow that could be seen from the windows. The odor of peat smoke was heavy in the air. Jodell walked up to the door and knocked. The door was ajar and opened wider when he knocked. He pushed the door open all the way so he could see inside. He walked in and gestured for Katrill to follow him.

The cabin was a small one. There was only one bedroom to the left of the door. The living room doubled as a dining room and kitchen. There was no furniture in the cabin except an old chair with two broken back legs that had been leaned against the wall. The fireplace was small but adequate for the size of the cabin. It was placed in the north wall. A huge black caldron hung in its opening, filled with dust. The floor was a dirt floor and there was an old carpet in front of the fireplace.

Jodell stood in the middle of the floor and scanned the room. It was certain no one had lived there for a long time, yet someone had been there recently.

"It seems we are alone here," Katrill said. Jodell nodded in agreement. The ashes in the fireplace were still smoldering, black smoke drifting up the chimney. This was the smoke he

30

had seen earlier and that attracted him to the cabin. Jodell checked the house and the grounds, but found no one.

"Did you find anything?" Katrill asked when he returned.

"No," Jodell answered cryptically.

"It is as I thought." Katrill looked around, testing the air with his fingers.

"What do you mean?" Jodell asked.

"I'm not sure yet," Katrill answered.

Jodell started a fire in the fireplace with dry logs he found just outside the cabin door, stacked in a neat pile. He removed the caldron from its hanger and started a small meal.

Winter was coming so the days were getting shorter. It was already nearly dark. The horizon was completely covered in shadow and seemed to creep up on the little cabin. Rain was just beginning to fall in a light drizzle. Lightning brightened the landscape as the storm moved closer. Jodell sat before the fire and cleaned his sword while Katrill lay back on his blanket, a cup of hot wine steaming at his side.

The evening turned to night and the rain came down in torrential force. The rain beat against the cabin almost drumming a tune against the aging wood and mud roof. Intermittent flashes of lightening lit the cabin with a bluish-white light, casting long leering shadows on the walls and leaving deep-shadowed corners. Neither man spoke to the other as the night progressed.

It was near dawn, the rain let up slightly, but still came down in a thick blanket of water. Jodell managed to fall asleep but tossed uncomfortably under his blanket. The fire burned low, crackling and hissing as drops of water fell into it from the chimney. Katrill sat up, his back to the fire, his staff leaning against his left shoulder, facing the door.

Something was wrong—Katrill could feel it, lurking just outside the cabin door. He steeled his nerves and prepared himself. It was that same aura that he'd felt earlier. It had remained just outside of his senses, only brushing lightly against his senses. He knew something was there but could not determine what or who.

Now the presence was stronger. He waited, his mind poised to attack or defend. Jodell stirred at his side but did not wake. He mumbled something and turned over, still clutching his sword. Katrill sat unmoving for what seemed like hours. He kept his eyes on the door, ears searching every corner of the cabin.

Suddenly a bolt of lightning struck the window, shattering the glass across the cabin floor. The cabin door flew open, a tremendous gust of wind rushing in. Katrill was picked up and thrown across the room, slammed against the back wall. Blue and green sparks flew from the impact of his shield against the wall. He still had his staff in his hand. The serpentine head was aglow with a bluish-white shimmer. A burst of efflorescent energy burst from the staff and shot across the room. There was a blinding explosion as it was met by a burst of blood red energy. Katrill's bolt was shattered into a million sparks. Another bolt of energy shot from the doorway, hitting Katrill in the chest. His shield flared bright blue. He was thrown against the wall again, the breath knocked out of him.

Jodell was on his feet, his sword in his hand. He squinted his eyes against the blinding light and flashes of power. Another bolt of energy shot toward Katrill. Jodell jumped, his sword extended into the path of the bolt. He screamed as energy raced down his arms and flew into his body. His arms burned as if they were being dipped in hot acid. His body burned as if a fire raged in his gut, his blood felt as if it was boiling.

Energy flowed through his body into his head, building up behind his eyes, burning like hot tongs being pressed against the inside of his eye lids. The pressure built up until he could no longer contain it—could no longer keep his eyelids closed. He screamed as his eyes flew open. Twin bolts of scarlet red energy burst from his eyes in continuous beams. There was a deathening scream and explosion as the entity was hit with the blast.

Shock waves raced through the cabin. All windows were blown out. The door was torn from the hinges. The walls of the cabin scorched black from the heat. Thick clouds of dust filled the cabin air.

Then it was over. As quickly as it started, it had ended. Jodell lay sprawled on his back, his eyes rolled up into his head. His face had been scorched from the heat of the confrontation, the rims of his eyes were burned and blistered. Both eyes were swollen nearly shut. His hands were covered with blood and blisters from the severe burns. Most of his clothing was burned away. He lay on his back, his breathing shallow and labored.

Katrill lay in a crumpled ball in the corner, consciousness coming back to him slowly, except for the ringing in his ears and a numb pulsing sensation in his chest and arms, he was otherwise unhurt. His shield had protected him from the first blast. Nothing would have saved him from the second. Jodell saved his life by jumping in front of the blast and taking the full brunt. By all rights he should be dead. Not only did he survive the blast, absorbing the energy and rechanneling it through his eyes, but he effectively turned their attacker's own energy blasts against it.

Katrill sat for a few moments allowing his head to stop spinning and think about what just transpired. He had never heard of anyone channeling energy through his eyes, especially energy of that magnitude.

Katrill crawled over to Jodell, placing his hands on both sides of his temples. He closed his eyes and willed himself to relax and enter Jodell's mind. He nearly broke his mind link as he felt the intensity of the pain in Jodell's mind. He had to delve deeper to reach his pain centers. He saw Jodell's life flashing as he went deeper. He saw the fight with Knub and his cohorts and was impressed with the speed and faculty with which Jodell dispatched them. He continued to go deeper. He saw all the things Jodell had run into on the road. He saw images of a little girl, a small delicate little thing with long flowing black hair and magical eyes. Still he needed to go deeper, but somehow he could not. Even in his weakened unconscious condition, Jodell's mind was strong enough to prevent him from going any deeper.

Katrill withdrew to the first level of consciousness and scanned Jodell's body for injuries. Aside from the blistering of his eyes and the burns he received on his hands, Jodell seemed alright, just badly shaken.

Katrill sat down beside Jodell, his mind still spinning. He closed his eyes. He needed rest, his energy reserves were badly depleted. But the cabin was no longer safe. Someone wanted them dead and sent a very powerful adversary after them. They had been fortunate and survived. He knew this would only be the first in a series of assaults to come. He was an experienced sorcerer and knew that next time they might not be so lucky.

The rain stopped completely. The sky was black and the air was still, damp and unusually calm. The odor of power was still in the air and reeked with the stench of corruption.

The night sky was starless and blank like a sheet of apprentice's lambskin paper. Huge pools of water stood outside the cabin as if the entire storm had been concentrated around this small cabin. Katrill made his way over to the power blackened doorway. He braced himself against the remnants of the door and looked out into the black night.

How calm the world seemed now. How empty and lonely the sky was. A desolate wasteland filled with dark wonders and alluring mystical treasures. He loved the night, the darkness and stillness that prevailed when the sun left the world and darkness wrapped itself around all living things.

The night was a time of power. He well knew the potential power that could only be performed at night when the stars were hidden behind the black canopy of midnight clouds. He had been attracted to those arts just like his friend, Jebeialle, but had found the strength to resist the temptation.

His friend had not proven to be so strong and had been caught up in darkness. Now he was on a mission to find and kill his friend before he became too powerful and nothing could stop him. He was old now and could not command the power as well as he once could.

He was a sorcerer of light, he practiced his arts in daylight and was as such limited. Jebeialle was also a sorcerer of light and those powers were addictive. It would take more than he could muster to defeat him. But Jebeialle became more powerful every day with each young life he stole. If he were not stopped soon . . . Katrill shook his head at that thought and walked back into the cabin.

Jodell still lay on his back, his head still resting on the hilt of his sword.

The new day was slow in coming. The night had not wanted to relinquish its hold over the world. Finally, dawn broke, pushing the darkness back over the horizon behind the distant Caverill Mountains. The air seemed to shimmer with residual energies still. All around the cabin was a nearly invisible dome of energy that had not yet dissipated. Katrill could feel the energy, raw and potent.

He shook his head determined not to dwell on what happened the night before. He was still badly shaken and had not been prepared for that attack, though he knew he should have been. He was a highly skilled sorcerer and had nearly been killed because of carelessness. He would not make that mistake again, he promised himself.

Jodell still lay on his back, his eyes hidden behind his swollen blistered eyelids. Katrill knelt down beside him putting his hand on his forehead. Jodell was feverish and in his weakened state, might not be able to pull through. He placed his hands on Jodell's temples, closing his eyes and concentrating. He slowly formed the link necessary to enter Jodell's mind. He became aware of the pain that still filled Jodell's mind and body. He pushed the discomfort to the back of his mind. His task now was to find the cause of his fever and bring it down.

He found what he could not find before. The sudden surge of power in his head inflamed the lining of his brain causing water to build up between his skull and brain. He had not been prepared to handle such a power surge.

Katrill withdrew knowing that Jodell would die if he didn't find a physician soon. There was nothing he could do for him except pour some of his own life's energies into him which could help Jodell to hold on a little while longer. But even that would not help for long.

Katrill fixed himself a small meal and fed Jodell a little hot spiced wine. He made a litter from the charred remains of the door and tied it behind Jodell's horse. He wrapped Jodell securely and tied him down in the litter. He left the cabin around noon that day, heading back southeast.

Five

The day passed uneventfully. There were intermittent bursts of showers but these were light and of short duration. Jodell woke to a semiconscious state several times during the day, babbling incoherently. Katrill wasn't much better, nodding in the saddle as he rode.

The sun went down before noon and the air chilled considerably. Beads of water sprinkled through Katrill's hair and ran down his neck to soak his collar. Strands of hair were plastered to his face. He shivered in the saddle as the cold penetrated his damp clothing. He wanted to stop and build a fire to warm himself and Jodell, but dared not. He needed to keep going as long as there was enough light to see. Sooner or later he had to run into a settlement or small village where Jodell could get some medical attention. So he kept going, trudging through the deepening mud.

Darkness finally came and Katrill made his camp amongst a small grove of spruce, situated on a small hill. From there he could see the surrounding valley on all sides and watch for anyone approaching. The trees provided a small measure of shelter from the steadily falling drizzle. The slope of the hill served to drain off the water so that the ground where he made his camp stayed relatively dry. He built a small fire and laid Jodell beside it to keep him dry and warm. He then opened his travelling sack which he carried across his back, and removed four rings. Two of silver and two of gold.

The first silver ring held a large blood red ruby, the second silver ring held a circular stone of onyx. The third ring, which was gold, held a small flawless emerald and the fourth ring, which was also gold, held a large sky-blue sapphire. Katrill paced off a square around his camp that was one hundred feet from each corner to the center. At each corner he placed a ring, pushing them into the ground so that only the stones shown. He placed the silver rings so they were opposite each other, and the gold ones so that they were opposite each other.

He plunged the end of his staff into the center of the fire so that it stood upright in the ground. The flames licked up the sides of his staff but didn't burn. He touched each ring in turn, starting with the ruby crossing over to the staff, touching the serpentine head and then touching the onyx stone. Again, he touched the staff then the emerald, the staff, the sapphire and again, the staff. He sat before the fire crosslegged, closing his eyes and visualizing what he had just set up. He concentrated on the staff, drawing strength from the light of the fire and spoke softly to himself.

"Begin." Each stone began to shimmer. The ruby, a deep scarlet red, the onyx, a shimmering fluid black, the emerald, a sparkling aqua green, and the sapphire, a pale powder blue. Katrill extended both his arms out to his sides and slowly raised them, bringing them together over his head. Red, black, green and blue power arched up from each stone to meet in a confluence point just above the staff, which was now glowing a soft, silver white. Katrill brought his hands down in front of his face, pointing his steepled fingers at the staff and spoke.

"Prime." A sparkling silver beam shot straight upward to connect with the confluence. Power flowed outward horizontally from the beams to form a dome of protection over the clearing. Katrill glanced around, satisfied with his work. He closed his eyes again and spoke the final word, "Set."

The shimmering dome disappeared. Katrill laid out his sleeping blanket and was asleep almost as soon as his head hit the ground, exhausted from his labors.

*   *   *

Katrill's mind churned restlessly. He was dreaming that someone was holding him and hitting him in the face and for some reason, he could not move or defend himself. Finally he woke and opened his eyes. Water was dripping from a leaf over his head into his face. He smiled to himself at the realizationi of the cause of his nightmare, but made no attempt to move. He lay where he was allowing the water to drip on his face and slowly drain down to end in a small silvery pool in his ear. He lay there for long moments as his mind cleared of the last vestiges of sleep.

Katrill had not allowed himself to think much about the events of two nights before. He wanted to try to put it out of his mind for a while. He had come so close to death and that had been frightening. He thought he had a handle on his fear. He thought himself prepared to make the sacrifice of giving up his life for what he believed, but was surprised to find out how hard it was to actually make that sacrifice when the time came. That was not his only concern, however. That confrontation had shown him just how old he had actually become. He thought himself prepared for the task. He knew that he alone would not be a match for Jebeialle even though he thought himself equal to anything else he would come up against. To find out that he was getting old and his power slipping was a shock to him. It was something he did not want to contemplate.

It was not yet fully light though dawn was breaking through the storm clouds that were still slowly receding to the east. Streaks of yellow-orange light formed long lean fingers that scratched at the bleak storm-darkened sky. A heavy mist hung low to the ground and hissed as vapors turned to steam from the brightly glowing embers of Katrill's fire. It was a couple of hours yet before the new day arrived. Katrill closed his eyes and allowed himself to doze off again.

*   *   *

Katrill came across a small town, which could be more correctly described as a small mud village. Children were playing in the muddy tract of a street and bolted into hiding when they saw him. He had been riding all morning and most of the afternoon and had not stopped to eat. The aroma of fried chicken and freshly baked black bread made his mouth water as he became painfully aware of his empty stomach.

His black gown was now a dirty shade of pale grey from the mud splatterings that caked the hem and sides nearly to his waist. His long silvered hair was likewise well caked but that did not bother him at his point. His mind churned with apprehension over Jodell's condition and his own pitiful state. It had taken him fourteen days to find a settlement in this backland country and every minute was precious for he did not know how long Jodell had left.

Katrill was responsible for Jodell and had he been more careful, Jodell would not be fighting for his life right now. He had been entrusted by the high counsul to protect and teach Jodell, to serve as mentor, protector, and friend. Instead of protecting Jodell, Jodell nearly died protecting him. What kind of protector was he if he caused the death of the one he was to protect? The counsul had chosen him as much out of the fact that he was a formidable sorcerer, as for the reason, he was familiar with Jebeialle and knew him better than anyone else. Everyone was depending on him and already, he was trying to fail. But he could not allow that to happen, he could not fail. He was half asleep in the saddle. His mind churned with his own inadequacies and made his spirit falter.

Katrill's horse trotted slowly through the heavy mud street pulling Jodell on his litter behind him. Katrill was only vaguely aware that his progress was painfully slow. He was deathly tired and his mind began to shut down from exhaustion.

Katrill felt a gentle tugging and a soft gentle voice seemed to enter his head and soothe him. The voice was consoling and gentle. Soft words caressed his mind, urging him to let himself go, to give in to its gentle care—he did.

He felt himself falling but could not help himself. His head spun and his eyes fluttered as he tried to catch himself, but his body would not respond. His muscles were too exhausted and his energy reserves too low. He relaxed and waited for the fall that was inevitable, but somehow never came. He was still falling, he knew, but somehow more slowly. He again felt that gentle voice in his head, soothing, reassuring.

The voice reminded him of his mother. That struck a chord of pain in him and he wanted to cry for her. He was alone in the world, a little boy only eight years old, all alone against the world and he was frightened. He wanted to run and hide from the world.

He felt a gentle touch on his cheek, that soothing voice in his head telling him he was safe and suddenly, he wasn't afraid. He felt himself being carried and he curled up in his mother's arms, laid his head on her soft breasts while her familiar perfume permeated the air. He slept the most peaceful slumber he had ever slept.

* * *

Katrill woke to the violent rumblings of his stomach. He was desperately hungry. He started to open his mouth and cringed a little from the sharp pain on his cracked dry lips. He licked them soothingly, tasting the slightly salty taste of his blood. He lay still for a few moments more, until he brought his racing heart under control. He became aware of a presence near him and opened his eyes. His vision was blurred as if he was looking through a half-frosted window. He closed his eyes on the rocks that scratched at them. His head still churned and felt light while his body felt leaden, his throat and chest, dry and hollow. He tried to take a deep breath and began coughing.

"Are you alright?" A light sweet voice said to him from the side of the bed. "Here, drink this, you'll feel better." Katrill opened his eyes and allowed them to focus on that voice. Beside him on a little stool sat a beautiful young girl of twelve. Her small black eyes darted across Katrill's face, her concern for him showing.

"Come on, Mister, you must drink this, it will make you feel better." She helped him sit up and brought a small wooden cup to his lips. A very fragrant tea steeped in the cup, sending plumes of white steam up Katrill's nose.

"Come now, you must drink it all," the girl admonished. "It's good for you, you know." Katrill managed a wry smile as he looked at her again.

"So you keep telling me," he said softly.

"There," the girl said after he'd drank it all down. "You'll be better in no time. You must lay back and rest now, I'll bring you some food later." She pressed him gently back into his pillow, drawing the heavy blankets up around his shoulders.

"Where am I?" Katrill asked.

"Now, now. No questions just yet. After you're rested, there will be plenty of time for that. Right now the thing for you to do is rest." The girl went over to the small fireplace, placed in the south wall and stirred the seething embers. She placed a few more logs on the fire working it until it roared again.

"There, that's better," she intoned as the warmth from the fire began to spread through the room. "That's better, don't you think so?" she said to Katrill with a smile.

"Very much better, thank you," Katrill answered.

"You sleep now and I'll look in on you later." She then left the room.

Katrill was awakened by the gentle pressure of small soft hands on his forehead. He opened his eyes and looked up into his caretaker's face and smiled. The girl smiled back warmly, her eyes aglow with life and youth and fascination. She turned her head and then spoke to someone else that Katrill had not been aware of.

"See, Mother, I told you he was improved. I took good care of him, just like you told me to." Her eyes flashed with pride with every word she spoke.

A tall, slender woman with long black hair that fell about her shoulders in heavy folds of curls, stepped up to the bed and peered over at Katrill. Her face was long and slender, her nose long and pointed. Her lips were rather full and sensuous. Her eyes were pools of ochre that picked up light from the embers in the fireplace and blazed with a subdued yellow-brown fire of their own.

Katrill stared up at her, drinking in her beauty as she felt his forehead and spoke to her daughter while absentmindedly tucking a thick curl back behind one ear.

"Yes, Cassie, you did a fine job, now go and finish setting the table."

"Okay, Mama," Cassie said and raced out of the room.

"She's a wonderfully beautiful child," Katrill said after Cassie left the room. "Just like her mother." The mother blushed and looked away from Katrill's face, a soft pretty smile forming on her lips.

"I see Cassie was right. you are improving." She smiled warmly as she spoke. "At any rate, you are too kind. Cassie's a nice girl and she tries too hard to please me. How are you feeling?" she asked Katrill after checking his pulse.

"Just fine now, I think, thanks to Cassie's ministrations. A little weak perhaps, but nothing a good solid meal won't take care of." Katrill sat up in bed while the mother helped swing his feet to the floor and helped steady him until his head cleared of vertigo.

"How's my friend?" Katrill asked, worry showing in his face.

"Don't worry about him, he's in good hands. He's at Mr. D'Indies house who's somewhat of a physician. He trained at the King's court for two years before his mother became ill and he had to come back to work and support her. It is lucky for us that he came back."

Katrill looked painful and grabbed her wrists. "How is he though, I must know, I'm responsible for him. If he should die, I could not ever forgive myself."

She looked at him and eased her arms out of his grip. "Don't worry, your friend will be fine. Mr. D'Indies is a very fine physician, he will do everything for him that he possibly can."

"You will let me know as soon as there is some news concerning his condition." She smiled at him and grabbed his hand, helping him to stand.

"Of course I will. However, right now, we must get you to the kitchen and get some hot food into you." Katrill smiled at that and went with her weakly into the kitchen.

*   *   *

The days passed slowly for Katrill. They had already been there for five days and his hostess firmly asserted that he and Jodell would be there for at least a week more. Jodell passed the crisis point during the first two days there and was rapidly improving. He was conscious now and his appetite was growing by leaps and bounds. Katrill became very friendly with his hostess. Cassie had taken to him immediately and made him her second father. He was fond of her as well, and was more than a little taken with her mother.

During the day, Katrill would cut wood for her and repair damaged portions of the house, as much to get her attention as out of gratitude for her helping them. In the evenings, he would sit with her for long hours, talking. They would discuss the day's work and Cassie. He told her about the world, the places he had been, and the things he had seen. She told him about her small, simple world. Often they talked late into the night. Cassie would curl up on the floor beside him and lay her head in his lap, staring up into his face, her eyes wide with awe and fascination at the stories he told, until she would fall asleep in his lap.

Katrill was happy here, with the simple, slow lifestyle Cassie and her mother lived. They led a life of innocence, a life away from the hatred and pain of most of the world. He wanted to share that innocence. Here he found a peacefulness he had only once ever come close to experiencing before. It was when he was a little boy and used to sit in his mother's lap and lay his head on her breast while she sang soft tunes to him until he went to sleep.

He remembered the sense of loss he'd felt when his mother died and he had to live with some relatives. Now again, he found that same peacefulness and did not want to leave.

Katrill had become attached to Cassie and her mother and it pained him deeply that he had to leave them. He constantly made up excuses why he could not leave them. He was too old to run around cavorting around the countryside like a young fool. It was time he settle down and raised a family. He tried to convince himself to stay, but his mind would drift back to his mission. He would have to admit to himself that he was being foolish.

One night, during one of their midnight talks before the fire, Cassie's mother brought his troubled thoughts to a head. She moved from her chair and knelt down beside him, putting her hands on top of his and spoke gently to him in the same gentle soft voice that helped him to sleep when he first arrived at their village, delirious with fever.

"Katrill," she began, her eyes ablaze with emotion, her long black hair framing her face in the soft light from the fireplace. "I know I'm a poor woman with little education." She continued, "But I could make you a good wife."

Katrill opened his mouth to speak, but she stopped him by putting her small fingers over his lips. "Please, don't speak now, let me finish. My husband, Cassie's father, died a few years ago. He was killed in the great war between Sartoe and Aldmere. Cassie was only six years old then and I was pregnant with our second child. I can still remember it as if it were yesterday. How I cried when he rode out to war. It was a bright spring day and the air was filled with the scent of honeysuckle."

She looked into the fire, her eyes staring blankly as she remembered. A tear rolled down the side of her face and fell on the back of Katrill's hand.

"I knew he wasn't coming back, that I would never see him again. I could feel it somehow. I knew that he would never see his second child. How I loved him then. I loved him so much."

She turned her face back to Katrill, tears streaming down her face now. She wiped her face with the back of her hand, still holding onto Katrill's hands.

"I felt it when he died. I was asleep and it was as if I heard someone call my name. I woke up in tears and I knew it was him calling to me. I knew he was lying in a field somewhere, dying. He needed me and there was nothing that I could do for him but cry." She stopped for a second, then continued.

"I lost the baby that night."

Katrill reached out and brushed back a loose curl that had fallen across her face. She pressed his hand to her cheek.

"The first year was the worst. After that, I was just numb. I swore that I would never love another man or remarry. But then I saw you the other day, you were sick and needed me and I loved you from the first moment." She buried her face in his hands and began to cry. He told her about his mission and how important it was to the world that his mission be completed.

"I cannot stay here, not now. Perhaps when this is all over," Katrill told her while holding her face between his hands. She looked into his eyes, stifling a sob and pulled him close, kissing him gently on the lips. He tasted the light saltiness of her tears as he returned her kiss. She drew him down onto the soft carpeted floor and spoke softly between kisses.

"You will come back to me after it's all over, won't you?" she asked.

"I will," Katrill answered.

"Promise me," she sniffed, still kissing his face and crying.

"I promise," Katrill said. They spent the night in each other's arms.

Jodell sat in his saddle and waited for Katrill to make his final good-byes. It had been nearly two weeks since they first arrived at the little village, and now it was time to move on. Jodell was mostly healed now except for a little residual blistering around his eyes that proved to be somewhat hard to heal. His memory of what happened that night was blurred and he made a mental note to ask Katrill about it. Katrill was kneeling, talking to Cassie who was crying.

"Please don't go. Don't leave us," she cried. Katrill was trying to console her, wiping at the tears that continually fell from her small black eyes.

"I can't, Cassie, I just can't. We went over this last night. I thought you understood."

"All I know is I love you and I want you to stay here with us, Mommy and me." Katrill looked up at that, to the mother who stood behind her daughter, her red-rimmed eyes testimony to the fact that she also had been crying.

"I'm sorry, Cassie. I can't stay, not now." Cassie began crying fervently and broke away from him, running into the house.

"Cassie, Cassie," Katrill called to her. He stood and grabbed the mother by the hand and kissed her lightly on the forehead.

"I have to leave now, Cerendi. Please talk to her, try to make her understand." She nodded yes. She didn't ask him to stay nor did she cry. She had done all that the night before while she lay cradled in his arms.

Katrill mounted his horse, turned and walked the horse slowly away. He didn't look back.

It was some time before he and Jodell spoke to each other. Katrill was still lost in his thoughts that lingered back at the village. Jodell respected his anguish and rode the rest of the afternoon in silence.

Katrill broke the silence himself, sometime just before nightfall. "I think, my friend, that we should begin to look for shelter for the night." Jodell acknowledged and found a large fir tree under which to make their camp. They had only traveled about ten miles that day, yet Katrill felt he could barely keep his eyes open. He rolled out his blanket, closing his eyes on his troubled thoughts.

The night was very cold. A frigid wind blew in from the north, slicing right through Jodell's heavy hide jacket. He pulled his cloak closer about his shoulders and moved closer to the fire. He sipped at a cup of hot wine and stared into the flames. He listened to the sound of the wood as it snapped and crackled in the flames.

Another sound came to his ears and he came to attention immediately. Another sound of a twig snapping caught his ear. At first he thought it was the wood in the fire. He had built enough fires to know the sound and it was not the same. He was sure he heard something from deep in the forest, moving steadily toward his camp. He sat unmoving, squinting across the fire, trying to see through the dense forest.

Katrill lay with his back to the fire, breathing with slow steady breaths. Their horses shuffled nervously on the end of their tethers. The hair on the back of Jodell's neck stood up as much out of anticipation as from the cold. He reached across his hip for his sword, it wasn't there!

There was a movement just at the fringes of the forest where it met the small clearing where they made camp. Jodell eyed his sword as it lay in its scabbard, draped neatly across a small bush where he laid it while cutting twigs to start his fire. It was too far away. He looked around for something closer. His eyes landed on Katrill's staff which lay beside him.

He pulled the staff to him slowly. The wood felt strange to his touch. The wood felt warm, his hand tingling as he touched it. He thought he saw a slight movement among the trees, a twig snapped. He grabbed the staff and stood up. The serpentine head flared a bright blue and exploded in a blinding flash of blue and red energy. Jodell was thrown backward a few feet from the force of the explosion. Katrill was instantly on his feet, his eyes wide with excitement. Jodell tried to stand only to stumble and fall again, still stunned by the force of the explosion.

"Someone across the clearing, look out!" He shouted to Katrill, who was still trying to stand. Katrill turned and looked—hazy blue light shimmered about his hands as he lifted them, ready to attack. His eyes went wide with shock as he extinguished his blue fire.

"Cassie!" he shouted as he recognized the girl coming across the clearing. She was crying as she came toward him. She threw herself into his arms, crying bitterly, her small body trembling from the cold.

"Cassie," Katrill said softly while hugging her. "What are you doing here?" She continued sobbing on his chest. He took off his riding cloak and wrapped it around her.

"Your mother must be half crazy with worry by now. Why did you try to follow me?" Cassie raised her head and looked at him from behind her tear filled eyes, still sniffling.

"I'm sorry. I just wanted to be with you." Katrill hugged her close, running his hands through her thick curly black hair.

"It's alright, sweetheart, everything is going to be alright," Katrill assured her.

The new morning found them heading back toward the little village. Cassie rode silently in front of Katrill. They had ridden a few miles when they came upon a search party looking for Cassie. Her mother was with them. When Cassie saw her, she raced to her, tears streaming down her face as they embraced. Cerendi and Katrill talked for a short while, made their good-byes again and parted.

They reached the end of the forest in three days, emerging at the barron flats of northernmost Sartoe. The air was cold and Jodell's feet were numb. The wind blew in from the mountains and sliced through his heavy jacket. His riding cloak kept him only marginally warm. He had to concentrate to keep his teeth from clanking together.

Jodell and Katrill rode side by side, heads bent low against the wind. It was late September now and the snows had not yet come. Jodell could feel the stinging bite of the moisture laden air and knew the snows were on the way.

The plains lay flat before them as far as the eye could see. They seemed to run into the base of the northern range of the Caverhill Mountains, which arched up into the sky, their huge snow-capped peaks disappearing into the clouds.

The Sartorian plains were desolate, nearly barren wasteland that served as a natural buffer between the Kingdoms of Man and the troll kingdoms in the mountains. Jodell eyed those mountains with a certain familiarity. He had come this way before.

Darkness came fast. The cloudless sky became a starless moonless void. Katrill and Jodell made their camp underneath a nearly leafless, short, thickly truncked tree. One of the few varieties that were tenacious enough to attempt to grow in the arid coldness of the plains.

They stretched a tent across the low hanging branches making an ineffective shelter against the wind. The night winds howled and tore at the makeshift tent, but somehow it held. They built a small fire in the center of the tent and cut a small hole in the center top to allow the smoke to escape. They ate a small meal and drank healthy portions of hot spiced wine which helped warm them considerably. Both men sat before the small fire, the warmth welcome after the bitter cold of the day.

"My friend," Katrill said as he sipped his wine, savoring the deep spiciness. "Do you know me?"

"I only know who you say you are," answered Jodell.

"And you accept that?"

"It doesn't matter," Jodell answered as he sipped his wine. "You are who you are. For some reason, you have chosen to follow me and I accept that. I think you will tell me why when you are ready." Katrill nodded his head in agreement with Jodell's logic as he poured himself another cup of wine.

"My friend, I am ready now." Jodell turned his head toward Katrill looking into his eyes. The creases around his eyes had deepened visibly since he first joined Jodell. His mien was

51

serious. Dust had settled into the lines etched in his face and made him appear older.

"I'm listening," Jodell said.

"I told you about Jebeialle, how he was a classmate of mine, a member of my clan. I was a very promising young Thermaurage. I learned my lessons fast and well. By my sixteenth month, I was already as good as he. By the end of my second year, I had surpassed him in skill, though he had been there for four years already." He stopped for a moment, then continued.

"I was appointed to a position that Jebeialle thought should have gone to him. After that, he became distant and grew more so every day. Nothing I said was right. He became belligerent and seriously hurt a new member of the order. He was reprimanded and that, in his eyes, was the final insult." He stopped talking long enough to take a long drink of wine.

"He broke into the most sacred chamber and stole some old parchment manuscripts. Those manuscripts were part of a secret find from an expedition to the city of the ancient ones. No one, except for the senior members of the high consul, was even supposed to know of their existence. We still haven't discovered how he found out, however, that's not important now."

"What was written on those scrolls?" Jodell asked.

"Those were the sacred scrolls of the Rites of Darkness."

"And what does all this have to do with me?" Jodell asked. "I get the feeling that you are trying to involve me in this thing."

"Ah, my young friend, you are the key to the entire thing."

"How so?" Jodell inquired.

"The Hated One is using those scrolls to increase his power. He is mad with power and seeks to dominate the world. We cannot allow that to happen."

Jodell looked at him skeptically. "I still fail to see what all this has to do with me."

"It has to do with your daughter." Jodell's eyes opened wide with that. He stood up and walked toward Katrill threatening.

"Old man," he said in a harsh vicious voice. "Watch what you say next." He stood up glaring down at Katrill. "What has this to do with my daughter?"

"If you will sit down and stop blocking the heat, I will finish telling you," Katrill said in an almost playful tone still sipping his wine.

"Alright, go on," Jodell said.

"The scrolls hold the secret of the powers of the darkness, the powers of the night. The power that is bound up in the dark heavens at night. That power which is inherent in a full moon that rolls out of the distant horizon like a heavy seaborne fog. Those scrolls hold the secrets of earth power, the darker side."

Katrill stopped talking and lay back sipping his wine. He looked up into the starless sky, sighing heavily. "He has to drink the blood of children and capture their souls. When he wants to use his newfound power, he is actually drawing life energy from those imprisoned souls. His victims are little girls of a certain age and are chosen special because of their peculiar type of innocence."

"And my daughter?"

"She met the criteria." Jodell sat and listened calmly for a few seconds before he spoke again.

"Then I can assume that my daughter is dead." Katrill dropped his head and nodded. Jodell turned to him with tears in his eyes.

"Then why is it that I can feel her presence? I can sense her somewhere, not too far away."

"That is why you are so important in all this. There is something special about you. You are a natural sorcerer. You were born to be a sorcerer."

"What are you talking about, old man?" Jodell asked incredulously. "You talk like a fool."

"Perhaps you are right, perhaps I am a fool. But that doesn't matter. What does matter, in fact, is that you can feel your daughter's presence because you and her have this ability and her blood calls out to you."

Katrill looked at Jodell, his eyes almost pleading. "You are special, my young friend. The type of natural sorcerer that comes about only once in a lifetime. You are our only hope to defeat the Hated One. If you refuse us now, the world is lost."

"And how about you, what is your part in all this?"

"I am to serve as your tutor and protector until such time as you are ready to face the Hated One."

"Why doesn't your clan just combine their powers and destroy him?" Jodell asked.

"It cannot be done. We are all sorcerers of the light, and our powers cannot be combined. However, he is skilled in both the powers of the darkness and the light and those powers can be combined."

Jodell thought for a few seconds and began to shake his head. He was a simple man who believed in few things. He believed in his ability to kill, his skill with a sword. He believed in his love for his daughter and his hatred for that person that abducted her. But he had difficulty believing in magic. He could not refute the fact that Katrill had shown some extraordinary abilities and had told him what he did in order to save his life. He could not explain what happened to him when he lifted Katrill's staff. But still, he shook his head, not wanting to believe what he was being told.

"No. I cannot accept what you are saying as truth. My daughter was abducted by some maniac, pure and simple. I will find him and kill him for that if it's the last thing I ever do."

"In that case, my young friend," Katrill said, his voice low with a hint of despair. "I'm afraid we are all lost and he has won." Katrill stretched out on his blanket before the fire.

"Good night, my friend," Katrill said, as he pulled the blankets over his shoulders. Jodell didn't answer but simply stared into the fire.

The next couple of days were cruel. The snow finally came. Four inches fell the first day. The temperature dropped and the wind picked up, whipping their riding cloaks straight out behind them.

The snow continued to fall and on the fourth day, turned to sleet. The wind whipped the sleet into their faces like the sting of a million tiny bees. At night it was worse, the winds picked up ever more and with the snow and no solid ground, they were not able to pitch their tent. Jodell was numb with cold. Already he could not feel his feet, yet he remained adamant and pressed on.

By the end of the sixth day, they reached the mountains. The wind died down to a quiet roar while the snow stopped. There was at least a foot or more of it now. It covered everything like a thick blanket of purest white sheeps' wool.

The mountains served as a buffer against the fierce north winds. The base of the mountains were not as heavily covered with snow. The mountains themselves rose high into the sky like huge white knuckles and brushed the wispy white clouds aside. The mountains lay in a group of three rows, each one successively taller than the first.

Jodell made his camp at the base of the mountain under a low outcrop of snow-laden rock that formed a natural shelter and fell just short of being a cave. He hung a heavy blanket over the opening, tied the horses in back of the natural cave and built a fire. He and Katrill huddled about the fire absorbing the heat, tentatively moving joints stiffened by the searing cold.

It was nearly dark when they first head it, low and muffled by the howl of the winds. As it got darker, the sound grew louder until Jodell could recognize it.

"Listen," he said to Katrill as he angled his head toward the sound.

"What is it?" Katrill asked as he instinctively reached for his staff.

"Don't you hear it? Those drums." Katrill listened for a few seconds, he could just barely hear the low muffled beat, the sound carried by the wind.

"Yes, I hear it now, what is it?"

"Rock trolls," Jodell said as his hand unconsciously rubbed the golden hilt of his sword. "They live in the valleys between the mountains. They're celebrating. I feel sorry for someone."

"Are we safe here?" Katrill asked.

"Quite. They will not hunt the plains while the storm keeps up. They generally stay high in the mountains and in the valleys between."

Jodell began gathering his things, preparing to move again. "It is time we moved out. The trolls sleep in the day and prowl at night. We will do the same. I will not be caught sleeping by a hungry troll." He had been talking while preparing to leave. Katrill didn't move from his position before the fire.

"Not we," Katrill said. "You. I will not go any further. You must go on alone from here. What you seek is waiting for you in the black tower just beyond the mountains."

"The black tower?" Jodell said questioningly. "How is it you know what I will find. I was under the impression you had never been here before."

"I have not," Katrill answered. "However, I know what you shall find just the same. You will not need me. I shall wait here for you to see if you have changed your mind."

Jodell opened his mouth and started to protest but then thought better of it. "As you wish, old man. As you wish."

Six

Jodell found the small path that wound through the mountains fairly easily. It was exactly as he had remembered except for the thick layer of snow. The pass was an opening about three feet wide between two mountains. The mountains towered on both sides, hundreds of feet into the air. Even though it was well past midnight, he was still able to see rather well.

The moon was out and shone brightly in the clear mountain air. The clean white snow caught the soft white moonlight, amplified it and reflected it, a billion miniature stars stretched out along the path and on the sides of the mountain walls.

The pass wound this way and that, angled up sharply and dropped off steeply. Jodell struggled against the slippery snow, scrambling up the steep snow- and ice-covered slopes and sliding back down the other side.

The pass emptied out onto what could not properly be called a road, but served the same purpose. It wound its way down the side of the mountain to the snow-covered valley below.

In the middle of the valley sat the hide tents of the rock trolls. Jodell hid behind the tents peering into the center of the circle formed by the tents. It was a small clan of only about fifty trolls, females and children included. The trolls were fierce fighters with two or three times the strength of a man. They were shorter that the average man, but well built with massive arms and legs. Their huge heads were thick skulled and their mouths displayed a large double set of canines. Their hands were huge with thick nails that were just short of being claws. Their eyes glowed a vicious canine yellow. They were very formidable foes in hand to hand combat. Their only redeeming quality was that they weren't very agile. A well-trained human with a sword or good battle-ax could hold his own.

Jodell didn't want to have to fight them. He was tired and cold and there were too many of them. He would have to wait until just before dawn when they were asleep and try to sneak past them. He settled down beneath a small out-cropping of rock where he had a good view of the entire camp and waited.

As the first rays of light flowed over the edges of the mountains, Jodell stirred. Dawn was eminent though it was still quite dark. Jodell listened closely and could hear the deep guttural sounds of sleeping trolls, and in the background, the soft crackle of fire. He made his way around the camp. It would have been easier to walk through the middle of the troll camp for the snow had been trampled down and most of it melted from the small fires the trolls lit. He didn't want to run the risk of waking any of the trolls and thought it more prudent to skirt the encampment.

He made his way past the camp and was just about to make his way into the small pass on the other side when he noticed something different. From one of the tents, a fire burned brightly. Jodell's interest was pricked. Trolls were thick-skinned with a heavy coat of fur. They seldom burned fires for warmth and they were basically afraid of fire, their only use for fire being for cooking.

Jodell crept up to the tent and peered in. On the floor near the far wall lay a man. His hands and feet were bound with hide thongs. He was guarded by a massive troll whose back was to the opening and Jodell. He carried a spear in one hand and had a sword strapped to his side. His fur was a dirty snow grey and his odor prevailed over the semi-sweet smoke from the hickory wood that burned in the fire.

Jodell stood and watched for a few moments. He didn't want to leave the man there but he also did not want to kill the troll either. The body would be discovered and the mountains would be crawling with trolls looking for them. He knew he could not leave the man behind. He was very familiar with trolls and knew what the man's fate would be.

Jodell stuck his head through the opening. The other man saw him then, his eyes opened with excitement. Jodell drew his sword from its sheath. It was over in a matter of seconds. The decapitated body of the troll lay in a growing pool of thick, nearly black-red ichor.

"My God, am I glad to see you!" the other man was saying as Jodell cut his bonds. "You are indeed a sight for sore eyes." Jodell wiped his sword on a piece of hide carpet and resheathed it. His cold grey eyes looked into the man's rustic brown ones scoldingly.

"Shut up and come on." Jodell led the way. He slipped through the tent door and disappeared across the clearing into the pass, the other man close behind.

It was fully light when they stopped to rest. They were halfway through the pass by now. The day was beautiful. The sky was filled with fluffy clouds that hung low over the tops of the mountains, casting heavy black shadows on the cliff faces. The air was still and seemed a little warmer than the day before. Jodell sat on a small boulder to rest. He drew his sword and began sharpening its edge with a small piece of flint he carried.

"My name is Orda, eldest son of Ordura, wife of B'ytkara, Chief of the Harbotka. I am deeply in your debt for saving my life. I am your servant, sir." Orda stood before Jodell, his head bowed, his hands outstretched with his hands clenched into double fists.

"My name is Jodell. There is no need for you to thank me and I have no use for a servant. I only did what I'm sure you would have done for me had I been in your predicament." Jodell resheathed his sword.

"Why are you in these mountains this time of year," Orda asked. "People don't usually come here." Jodell stood and resumed walking up the pass, Orda falling in beside him.

"I might ask you the same thing," Jodell said. Orda's eyes glazed over as his thoughts turned inward.

"I search for my father. He came this way looking for my sister and had five men with him. That was twelve days ago, before the snows started. None of them have yet returned."

"And you search for them alone?" Jodell asked.

"There were four of us that started out. I lost one of them to the mountain, the others were . . ." Orda's voice trailed off as he remembered.

He and Jodell walked in silence. It was late afternoon when they emerged from the mountain pass. It opened upon a huge green valley. The grass grew tall and straight here to six feet or more and swayed gently on a soft breeze.

Here there was no snow. The air was warm and sweet with scents of honeysuckle and primrose. The valley stretched out for fifty miles or more before it ran into the base of the third row of mountains. There were no real trees, only what appeared to be huge stalks of grass as thick around as a man's thigh. Some stalks reached heights of ten feet or more but they were few and scattered.

The pass emptied out into the valley with a sheer drop of a few thousand feet. The snow behind them melted where it met the warmth of the valley and formed small waterfalls all across the face of the mountain.

"My God, what manner of place is this!" Orda was saying as he stood at the edge gaping out at the plain. Jodell took a deep breath, tasting the sweet mountain air.

"This is a paradise. A paradise in the midst of hell."

*　　*　　*

The tower rose into the sky and towered over the valley. There were three large windows at the very top and a smaller one a little lower down. There was no visible entrance that Jodell could see. He searched the entire base of the tower without finding so much as a crack in the seemingly solid stone.

The ground around the tower was also solid rock that eliminated the possibility of a trapdoor entrance. The tower had been chiseled out of solid rock and the stone had been left chiseled to a point so that near razor edges formed the sides of the tower. It would not be possible to climb up to the windows. Jodell stood back and contemplated the tower.

There must be a way in, he thought. *There must be.*

Orda was talking to Jodell who was engrossed in thought and had not heard him. "Hey, are you listening to me?"

Jodell blinked and looked at Orda, his expression changing to a more normal one. "I'm sorry, what were you saying."

"Are you okay?" Orda asked. "Your eyes are red." Jodell brought up his hands to his face and rubbed his eyes. They felt dry and a little irritated.

"I'm fine, just a little tired," Jodell said, returning his attention to the tower.

There was something here and he could feel it. There was a way to get into the tower but he didn't know how. It was getting late, evening was fast approaching. "Well, what do you think?" Orda was saying. "There doesn't appear to be a way in and it's going to be dark soon."

"We will just have to make a way in," Jodell answered.

By then it was getting dark. The mountains were lit with the faint reddish glow of individual fires of the trolls. The horizon was alive with reds and ochres and flickers of blue washed with a thin layer of frosted white.

The lush greenery of the valley seemed to glow as darkness settled in. Jodell could detect a faint, almost imperceptible shimmer that encapsulated the entire valley. He could not see it if he looked straight at it, but could catch a glimpse of it out of the corner of his eye. His nerves tingled and pulsed as he picked up gyrations of power. His skin crawled and his eyes burned.

The darker it became the more intense the sensations became. Jodell rubbed at the burning in his eyes trying to will himself to relax. He felt the power building behind his eyes trying to force itself out. He closed his eyes and sat down on the soft grasses at the base of the tower leaning against it. He willed his mind to relax, to quiet his nerves and concentrate on dispersing the tension in his brain. Finally the pressure eased and he felt the energy excess drain from him. His breathing returned to normal and he soon fell asleep.

*   *   *

Jodell woke to complete darkness, his eyes popping open. His hand was already on his sword hilt. His eyes searched the tall dark immersed grasses all around. He listened closely. Orda was stretched out beside him, his chest heaving up and down as he slept. Jodell nudged him with his knee. Orda groaned and rolled over, his eyes bloodshot from sleep.

"What is it?" Orda started to ask.

"Quiet," Jodell whispered as he drew his sword. "Listen." Orda sat up, his mind instantly alert.

"There," Orda whispered. "That way. Something's out there." He pointed.

"Quiet." Jodell repeated as he climbed to his feet taking a defensive stance, his back to the tower. Orda looked at him questioningly then drew his battle-ax cradled in the bend of his left arm.

The tall grasses parted and seven trolls stepped out into the clearing. They formed a semi-circle around Jodell and Orda. The two end trolls carried torches. They all carried clubs except for one, who carried a studded iron-shod mace in a gauntleted left hand. He was the largest of the trolls. He stood nearly as tall as Jodell but his massive arms and shoulders made him appear even taller.

They stood looking at Jodell and Orda for a few seconds. The gauntleted one who was clearly the leader of the group stepped forward, his huge eyes were red rather than yellow like the other trolls. His fur was a deep shade of dark brown and was shorter that the others. His uncovered hand terminated in a vicious set of talons a full inch long and half inch around. He could disembowel a man with one blow.

Jodell mumbled almost to himself, "Ogre."

The Ogre let out a deep guttural laugh that resounded throughout the valley. His massive canines reflecting the light from the torches.

"Ah, you are a well informed human, indeed." The Ogre's words were slurred as he spoke through his teeth. He bent deeply at the waist in mock curtsy as he introduced himself.

"I am Fandall, the slayer. I slay people." Jodell's eyes spat venom as he raised his sword point.

"And I am Imack, Elf friend and Ogre slayer." Fandall let out a mighty roar of laughter that seemed to shake the ground beneath Orda's feet. Fandall raised his mace and took a step forward.

"This one is mine," he spat. "No one . . ." Before he finished his sentence, Jodell attacked. He brought his sword up before the Ogre's face in a feint, then swung low, his sword biting deep into the Ogre's lower abdomen. Black-red blood and gore spilled out as the Ogre screamed and reached for his stomach. Jodell shifted his weight, pivoted and plunged his sword between the Ogre's shoulder blades, nearly up to the hilt. He twisted it and snatched it out, using his foot to brace the Ogre's chest. The Ogre hit the ground with a thump. Jodell turned and barely ducked the swing of a club. He cut at the legs of the attacking troll, his blade biting deeply and clanging against the massive leg bones.

Orda had already neatly dispatched two trolls and was circling a third. He feinted a charge, the troll swung wide with his club. Orda threw his axe. The troll tried to side step but was too slow. The entire head of the axe buried itself in his chest, his heart was split in two. Orda turned to look for other trolls. Jodell had finished off the fourth troll and stood over his body, watching the other two trolls. They stood where they were holding the torches, they did not join the fight. They stood there for a few seconds then turned to leave. Orda retrieved his axe and started after them.

"Let them go," Jodell said as he began to clean his sword on the grass.

"But they will go and bring the others," Orda protested.

"I think not. They will tell who I am and what has happened. I don't think we will be bothered again." Orda shrugged his shoulders and let them go.

"Why didn't those two fight?" Orda asked as he cleared his axe head and sharpened its edges.

"They were young trolls learning to be warriors. They were not permitted to join the fight," Jodell explained.

Orda finished his axe and returned it to its sheath. "I'm familiar with trolls, have had to deal with them before, but I have never seen a troll like that one before. My God, he was big."

Jodell resheathed his sword and looked up at the sky. It was nearly dawn now, there was a slight breeze blowing in from the south, and with it was the hint of dampness—possibly rain. The first trace of light was beginning to filter through the heavy shimmer that overlaid the valley. Heavy clouds scuddled across the sky from south to north, heavy water-laden clouds moving like defeated giants who had just lost a final battle.

"That was no troll, that was an Ogre. They are more intelligent than trolls and much more dangerous."

"I didn't know that those creatures lived in these mountains also."

"They do not, they are lowlanders. They live in the forests and marsh country of Aldmere."

"Then what the hell was he doing this far north?" Orda asked.

"That is a good question," Jodell answered.

"I would hate to run into a group of those," Orda was saying as he nervously fingered his axe. Jodell looked at him, his grey eyes distant and emotionless.

"Where there is one, there are others. Ogres never travel alone."

The day burst in on them with the full brilliance of the sun. The morning was hotter than the previous one. A heavy fog had settled in early but was being dispersed by the sun, forming small pools of water that wet the grasses and bent them under its weight. The air smelled fresh and invigorating, like newly cut grass. Jodell took on a new resolve and began searching the base of the tower again for an opening.

Jodell walked the full circumference of the tower which was only about three hundred feet around. On his third time around he stopped at a small indentation of rock. There was something different about this spot. He was not sure what it was. It was only a feeling he had, and even then he could not sustain that feeling for long. It was a sensation he felt when he passed that particular spot.

He stopped again but could not localize the sensation. He walked the circumference of the tower again and as he passed the spot again, he saw out of the corner of his eye a faint spark or sparkle, bluish-red and nearly imperceptible. He approached the spot, reached out his hand and touched it. He jerked his hand back as a surge of power shot through his arm, filled his body and knocked him off his feet, throwing him nearly fifteen feet backward. The air around the tower lit up, covering it in a translucent web of power.

Jodell lay stunned for a few moments, his left arm was nearly numb and the tips of his fingers were slightly blistered. Orda stood over him wiping water on his face from the wet grasses.

"Are you okay, you alright?" Orda was saying. Jodell opened his eyes and sat up as the lethargy left his body.

"I'm fine." He stood, somewhat shakily and walked over to the tower and stood, staring at it.

"What the hell did you do?" Orda asked. "Now we will never get in there."

Jodell stood back and threw a stalk of grass into the web—it vaporized. "So it would seem." Jodell turned and walked away from the tower, his face blank but his eyes smoldered. Orda followed him out of the valley.

Seven

The small cave was much the same as he left it—a little cleaner perhaps but still the same. A small fire burned in the middle of it and a pot of hot tea steeped over the fire. A small dish of roasted pork sat nearby, still warm, and a pot of steamed tubers sat beside it. The aroma aroused their hunger, set their stomachs rumbling. Orda looked about the small cave with a certain amount of appreciation.

The cave was pleasantly warm and the food smelled inviting. He sat down and poured himself a cup of tea. The flavor was deep and hearty and warmed his stomach pleasantly. He felt his muscles relax as the warmth flowed through him. He speared a slice of pork and grabbed a large tuber and slumped it down with a piece of bread he'd dipped in his tea. He licked the juice from his fingers as he speared another piece of meat and spoke between swallows.

"It seems someone was expecting us. Nice of him to prepare us a meal," Orda continued eating greedily. "You had better join me, this food is delicious."

Jodell stood looking out into the evening sky. It was dusk and the ground was getting dark, yet the sky was still a deep purple with smatterings of red and ochre. The last traces of sunlight danced on the horizon as it receded to the west, dipping slowly below the snow-covered plains of northern Sartoe.

Jodell stood with his eyes half shut against the brisk wind that blew in past the heavy hide blanket that covered the opening. His mind wandered. He had not been able to get into the tower and yet, he felt he must, somehow. He felt that there lay what he was searching for, he was sure of it. He felt that the answer lay with Katrill. He came back to the cave to find the old man gone. The horses were still there so he could not have gone far. He had fixed a meal which was still warm, so it could not have been long ago when he left. He would be back.

Jodell looked out across the snow. It had not been snowing for at least a day and yet there were no tracks in the snow, except for those he and Orda made. He wondered where the old man had gone.

It was dark when Katrill finally appeared. He carried a bundle of dry wood under his arm, along with a small jug of dark red wine. Jodell was still standing at the doorway when he appeared, listening to the beating of the troll drums.

"Ah, you are back now," Katrill said as he approached the doorway. Jodell had not been aware of his presence until now.

"Where have you been?" Jodell spoke in his usual dispassionate tone.

"I've been out," Katrill answered as he entered the cave. "Did you find what you sought in the tower?"

Jodell reentered the cave and for the first time, grabbed a piece of meat which was cold by then. "You know full well what I found, old man. Why did you play me for a fool?" Katrill grinned at him, then looked at Orda and offered his hand.

"This one is quite unmannered," he gestured at Jodell. "My name is Katrill." Orda looked at Jodell hesitantly. Jodell didn't look at him.

"My name is Orda."

"Yes, I know. You are Orda, eldest son of Ordura, wife of Bytkara, and prince of the Harbotka." Orda looked disturbed at that. He withdrew his hand and unconsciously gripped the handle of his axe.

"How do you know that?" he asked, puzzled. Katrill poured himself a cup of wine and drank deeply, sighing with appreciation.

I know many things," Katrill answered. "At any rate, you are welcome here." Orda bowed his thanks and didn't pursue the matter.

Jodell fingered a tuber and downed a cup of wine then spoke while looking into his cup. "Old man." His voice was serious with a slight edge to it that spoke of his agitation.

"Yes," Katrill responded.

"I need . . . No, I demand some answers from you and I want them now."

"To get answers one must ask a question, mustn't one?" Jodell looked up at that, his grey flecked eyes burning.

"Do not banter with me, old man, I am not in the mood. You knew how to enter that tower and kept it from me. I have a right to know." Katrill's mien fell, his posture becoming serious. His voice was raised slightly and his eyes met with Jodell's. His blue eyes seemed to burn a deep black-blue fire that originated from deep inside him. The whites of his eyes were red with anger and his knuckles were white where he gripped his staff.

"Don't you speak to me about rights. You haven't a right to anything. While you ride around the countryside looking for your daughter the world is falling apart. Because of your selfishness, people are dying at this very moment. Don't these people have rights, a right to live in peace with the ones they love? Do you think you are the only one who is hurting because a loved one is lost or dead? You sit here wallowing in self-pity while the whole world is dying and tell me you have a right. You haven't a right to anything."

Jodell stood and glared down at Katrill, his fists clenched at his sides. "Don't tell me about the hurts of the world, I owe the world nothing. The world has given me nothing but pain and anguish. I owe the world nothing at all. And who the hell are you to follow me around the countryside to get me to participate in some private war of yours that I know nothing about. I have my own problems to worry about without getting involved in the problems of the world."

Katrill stared into the flames for a few seconds then stood up slowly and turned to face Jodell. "You know you are absolutely right, you owe the world nothing and the world owes you nothing." Katrill turned and started to walk away. He heard the swish of Jodell's sword as it cleared its scabbard. He stopped and spoke without looking back.

"Savior of the world or not, I will not hesitate to kill you where you stand. You are no match for me, not yet." Katrill stood still, his back to Jodell, for a few long moments. Finally he heard the sword go back into its sheath. He walked away and left the cave. Only then did Orda allow himself to breathe.

After a while Orda followed Katrill out of the cave. He was standing out in the snow, his face lifted to the night sky, his eyes closed. Orda walked toward him, the heavy snow muffling his steps. The air was cold but mostly still and the snow had stopped falling. He cleared his throat as he approached Katrill to let him know he was coming. He stopped a few feet from him and looked up at the sky. Katrill opened his eyes and then spoke. His voice was calm without a trace of the emotion it held only a few moments ago.

"The sky's beautiful, isn't it."

"Yes it is, and so peaceful," Orda said.

"Yes, peaceful like death." Katrill responded. This disturbed Orda a little but he said nothing.

"The sky is dark, so beautiful and so cold. It holds so many dark mysteries, and yet is the source of all light, of all life. No matter what happens on this planet, the sky will always be there, cold and peaceful. No matter what we do, we cannot affect it. The sky, the heavens are the only constant in this chaotic world. Man may change the features of the land, change the course of the greatest rivers, even move mountains, but regardless of what he does the sky always remains the same."

Katrill turned to look at Orda, a pained expression in his eyes. "Forgive the musings of a stupid old man." He smiled at Orda. "I need to talk to you. Something has happened that concerns you and I think I should tell you now. Let's go back inside to the fire."

*   *   *

The three of them set out early the next morning. Orda rode with Jodell. His face was grim. His expression spoke of his feelings. His eyes were glazed over and stared at Jodell's back. None of them spoke, they simply moved at a slow trot. The snow started falling again, a soft cascade of white feathers that settled gently, turning the three of them white, like salt sculptures floating on a milk-white sea.

The snow ended after one day and the sun came out. The snow, which lay stretched out like a thick wool carpet, picked up the sunlight and reflected it. They had to squint their eyes against the brilliance of it and still they were nearly blinded.

Jodell didn't need to see to know where he was going. It was basically a straight line since the Sartorian plains were mostly flat country. They simply closed their eyes and let the horses guide themselves. Though the sun was bright, it added little warmth to the air although they were thankful for what little warmth it did provide. The slight pressure of sunlight against Orda's skin was welcomed as it allowed him something to focus his seething mind on.

The three of them rode on keeping mostly to themselves, only speaking when it was necessary. They rode during the day and tried to catch what sleep they could while riding.

There was no reason trying to make a camp, there was no shelter, nothing from which they could hang their tent. At night they lay out their blankets on the snow forming a rough circle, built a fire in the center and moved on the next morning.

It took them eight days to reach the edge of the plains. There they turned east and then south after half a day's ride. They followed a huge road that was once a major throughway before the great war, but now was a grim reminder of the glory that was once Sartoe. Sartoe had been at one time the mightiest nation among the seven kingdoms of man and the center of civilization. The road was now a minor artery that wound its way across the country, connecting all major cities, and ran all the way south to the port city of Dalmouth.

The Harbotka village was more a huge town than a village. It lay spread out at the base of a large hill and formed a circle around it. There were battlements built on top of the hill and a castle with an outer wall that ran completely around it. The wall had been built of pure granite blocks ten feet thick and ten feet wide. There was only one gate situated in the south wall. The gate was built of huge timbers that were no less than fifty feet tall.

The timbers were bound together by a thick band of iron at the top, bottom and middle. The gates were made to be lifted instead of swung open which added to its strength. Beyond the wall was a moat a full five hundred feet across at its widest point. It was a natural moat. Water bubbled up from somewhere deep within the mountain and ran somewhere else, forming a rushing circular river and a whirlpool where the water went out.

Beyond the moat was a second wall also of granite, an exact duplicate of the first wall. In the center of it all was the castle. From its embrasures the entire countryside could be seen for miles in all directions.

Katrill stopped his horse and Jodell pulled his up alongside. They stood atop a small hill where they could get a good view of the northern side of the town. The town was quiet. No smoke bellowed up from the chimney stacks. No children played out in the snow-covered streets. There were no guards along the walls of the fortress or in the turrets of the castle. The gates to the city were raised and the air hummed with an unnatural silence.

Jodell turned to Orda. "Are you sure you want to go? We could go instead."

Orda lifted his head, his eyes were glassy and tear filled though he held them back. "No, I'll go myself," he said simply. Jodell nodded and nudged his horse forward.

The full impact of the carnage didn't hit Orda until he entered the town. Frozen bodies lay everywhere, hanging from windows, lying out in the streets. The nude half-eaten body of a young girl lay impaled on a huge spear, her fearful eyes still staring. They searched the town for survivors—there weren't any.

Orda walked over to Katrill, his face ashen and his body shaking slightly. When he spoke his voice cracked. "I must check the castle, see if any of my family . . ." His voice trailed off.

Katrill placed his arm around the shorter man's shoulder in an effort to console him. "I think it better if you didn't. There won't be much left. The trolls are very thorough."

"No!" protested Orda. "I must go. I must bury my family. It is my responsibility and mine alone." He turned away, then headed for the castle. Jodell started after him but Katrill stopped him.

"No, my friend. Let him go. This is something he must face, and he must face it alone." Jodell stopped and looked at him for a moment then watched Orda as he disappeared up the street.

They made camp in a small house on the outskirts of town. Katrill started a fire in a small clay oven and heated up some wine. He didn't make any food because neither he nor Jodell were hungry. Jodell's mind churned at the senseless death and destruction left in the wake of the trolls. He had fought the trolls before and had seen the damage they could do, knew their potential for slaughter. His stomach churned at the thought of the little girl he'd seen. He took a long swallow of his wine, drained his glass and poured himself some more. He wanted to forget, needed to forget. She had been about the age of his own little girl at the time she was abducted. Her hair was long and black. Her eyes small and round and black like onyx.

Jodell drew in a deep breath and came out of his reverie. "What is happening, old man?" he asked Katrill.

"What does it matter now," Katrill answered. "What does it matter to you? You have decided that you owe the world nothing, so what's the use of talking about it?" There was a hint of despair in his voice, mixed with resolve. "It is not your concern."

"Katrill," Jodell called him by name and faced him. Katrill could not help but meet his eyes for he was shocked. Jodell never called him by his name before.

"First," Jodell continued. "First I want to apologize for the things I said to you and the way I acted at the cave. I have been thinking and I have decided that you are right and I am wrong. I'm being selfish and I realize that now. It's just that I've searched for my daughter for so long now and to get this close, so close it seems I can smell the fragrance of her hair. It is not easy for me to give her up."

"Do not apologize for loving your daughter. It is because of that special love you shared between you that makes you what you are. Love is like anything else, the more you practice it the better you get at it and the stronger you become as a result. In your case, that strength is expressed in your ability to command sorcery."

"I am ready to learn from you, to help you in your fight," Jodell said.

"You must not change your mind in order to please me. That would never work. You must do this for yourself, for the world and for your daughter. Mostly for your daughter. She will never be able to rest until you have avenged her. Because your love for your daughter transcends all bounds, it will allow you to withstand any magic that can be brought to bear against you. The thing you must learn, however, is that this is not just my fight but yours as well, and that you alone have the power to defeat our enemy."

Jodell nodded his acceptance. "When will the lessons begin, old man? I am ready."

"They have already begun," Katrill said as he sipped his wine. "They began the day I met you in the forest and have continued until now." Jodell nodded.

Orda returned shortly after midnight. His eyes were heavily glazed, a deep pain stabbed at his soul yet he shed no tears, showed no emotion. All of his emotions had been vented up at the fortress. He was left a hollow shell of a man, devoid of all emotion, all family and people. Neither Jodell nor Katrill spoke to him as he entered the house. He walked over to the window and looked out toward the castle. The entire horizon was aglow with the bright yellow and red light from the funeral pyre. The crackle of the fire came to them over the gentle night wind, bringing with it the smell of burning wood. Orda stood watching it for a long time.

The next morning was cold and dreary. The snow had resumed a slow, almost deliberate descent during the night and completely covered the carnage left by the trolls. Katrill was grateful for Orda's sake. After a small light breakfast, from which Orda abstained, they prepared to move on.

Katrill approached Orda who looked to be on the verge of total despair. His small round eyes were red-rimmed from sleeplessness and crying. Deep wrinkles etched themselves in the corners of his eyes and his color seemed pale.

"Orda, Jodell and I must be moving on. We have a lot to do and little time in which to do it. We wondered what plans you have. You are welcome to accompany us if that is what you wish." He stood there for a few moments but Orda didn't answer him or look at him, but simply stared at the ground.

"Well," Katrill continued after a moment. "I understand." He clasped him on the shoulder and walked away. "I'm sorry."

"Wait!" Orda called after him. Katrill turned and waited for him. "I have nothing left to keep me here and no place to go. Jodell has told me some of what you are attempting to do. What I want to know is why." Orda was beginning to show signs of a breakdown. Tears filled his eyes and his voice shook lightly.

"Why were my people murdered. I feel that magic is somehow the cause of all this. You are a magician, therefore, you must have some answers. Katrill, I need some answers, something to give my life direction."

"Come, ride with us," Katrill said as he put his arm around the shorter man's shoulders. "I will tell you all about it as we ride."

The three men rode until late afternoon before stopping to rest and eat. Katrill told them the entire story, leaving nothing out.

". . . And now it starts. The Hated One seeks the power stones of the elves beneath with these, he can fully acclimate his power and become the most powerful sorcerer in the world."

77

"But why start a war that will devastate the land?" Orda asked.

"The Hated One knows that we are searching for him. He knows that even though he has combined the powers of light and darkness, he is still missing that vital link, the power stones. He is powerful but so is the Council of Wizards. None of us knows just how powerful we are. A battle between two powerful sorcerers could be devastating, it could conceivably destroy the world."

Jodell spoke up then. "But that doesn't explain why he is starting this war. All he has to do is lay low while he searches for the stones. This war doesn't make any sense."

"Oh, but it does," Katrill explained. "He knows that if he starts this war, the Council's attention will be averted. It is simply a diversionary tactic. If the council has to spend its time coordinating a defense against his army, they cannot concentrate on finding him. And if he finds the stones before we do, the war won't matter."

"Can't he coordinate this war and look for these stones at the same time?" Orda asked.

"He has help with that. People who report directly to him."

"Who are they?" Jodell asked.

"I think you met one of them back at the abandoned farm. They are minor magicians from a lesser order. People who have a talent for sorcery but fall short of the ability it takes to become full senior sorcerers."

"If that was one of them back at the farm, he seemed awfully powerful to me," Jodell said.

"That's true," Katrill admitted. "He must be augmenting their power. We will have to be careful."

"So where do we go from here?" Orda asked.

"To the Valley of Shadows, and then to a place some call the City of Leaves."

"I've heard of that place but I've never been there. I have been to the Valley of Shadows. It was once a beautiful place, but now it's ogre country and not a pleasant place to visit." Jodell remembered better times when he was younger and the Elves still lived in their magnificent valley.

Katrill looked at him sidelong. "I know you've been there, you were well known there. The Hated One is using the ogres as officers in his army. We go to the valley to kill the ogre king." There was silence for a few moments as the other two men thought about that. It was Jodell who finally spoke up.

"That won't be easy. The ogres are very intelligent, nearly as intelligent as men. They will be guarding."

"That's true," Katrill said. "However, it must be done. If we kill the king, the ogres will not fight, at least not coordinately. They will be busy fighting among themselves. We start a power struggle. That will disrupt some of the leadership in the Hated One's army, cause him trouble and slow him down. Thus giving us more time to find the stones." Katrill stopped his horse and looked up at the sky, it was getting slowly darker. It was late evening and night was on its way, it was time they started looking for a camp site.

"If either of you want out of this, this is the time to do it. When we get to Dalmouth it will be too late to change. The Hated One will have agents there watching us." He looked at Jodell.

"You have already experienced the power of one of his agents, so you understand the seriousness of what we are up against." He looked at each of them for a reply. Orda finally spoke.

"I'm with you all the way. I have a little debt to repay."

"Good," Katrill answered as he looked at Jodell.

"I have not changed my mind. I go with you."

"Then I suggest we find a site to make camp for the night and try to get some rest. We enter the city tomorrow."

Eight

The city of Dalmouth was a sprawling metropolis situated at a confluence of two rivers that emptied into a huge lake that looked more like a sea. It was a harbor town and like all harbor towns, was a rich city. Wealthy merchants walked along the streets with their body guards, dressed in fine silks and gold embroidered velvets and satins.

The streets of the city were lined with tents and stalls selling every conceivable item. One stall sold fresh pastries while next door a fat man sold young girls. The city was a melting pot of races. People came here from all over the seven kingdoms to buy and sell. Jodell walked through the streets with an air of detached resentment.

He had been here before but that was before the great war. The city had been different then somehow. The streets were the same and the buildings were basically the same. Even then the city had been a rich port town with many races of people, yet now something was changed. It was nothing he could put his finger on, nothing he could see or put into words. It was a feeling he had, a sensation that picked at his ever more sensitive nerves. There was something in the air, an odor or a haze that he could not smell or touch, but he could taste it; taste it with his senses and it tasted foul, corrupt like a gangrenous wound that would not heal.

The stench of corruption was so strong that Jodell found himself holding his breath, trying to keep it out, but he couldn't. He, Orda and Katrill walked along the harbor toward what was considered the center of town even though it wasn't the geographic center. It was where huge luxurious inns and pubs catered to the rich merchants and lords of the city. It was where the best rooms could be found and the finest of foods and wines.

The three of them were tired and haggard looking and were not in the mood for having to watch every cutthroat they came across. They decided to get rooms at a rather expensive-looking inn called the River's Edge Inn and Pub, as the sign so proudly proclaimed.

"What do you think?" Katrill asked Jodell.

"It is generally the best inn in town," Jodell answered. Orda was looking around at the richly but sparsely dressed women that passed him, some of them managing to accidentally brush him and pretending complete innocence while enticing him with their eyes.

"Well, if nothing else, the view is beautiful," Orda observed, smiling. "Look, you two go in, find rooms and get something to eat. I'll be back later."

"Orda," Katrill called after him. "Be careful."

"Yeah, I will. Don't worry," Orda answered as he walked away.

"He can handle himself in a fight," Jodell said to Katrill as they entered the inn. "He'll be okay."

The first floor of the inn was a huge dining hall with large glass top tables. The walls were of the finest hand-carved mahogany, polished to a glistening shine and trimmed in burnished gold and silver leaf. The ceiling was hung with huge copper chandeliers and burned the finest scented oils and illuminated the hall with a hazy purple-blue that reflected from the polished marble floors—itself a work of art.

There were serfs polishing the walls, floors and furniture at all times. The entire east wall was glass that overlooked the point where the River of the Seven Virgins and the River of Glass came together and emptied into the Lake of the Lords.

Jodell found a well-polished table near the rear wall in a corner that faced the glass wall and offered a splendid view of the lake. There were hard rolls and butter with honey and milk already on the table. He began to eat. Katrill went to the counter where the inn manager was and requested rooms.

"That will be two gold coins per person per night and meals are extra. If you want hot baths, that's extra, too."

"That's awfully expensive just for a room," Katrill said as he reached for his purse.

"This is an expensive place. If you want cheap, go some place else." The manager retorted sarcastically as he held his hands out expectantly. Katrill brought out two gold coins and placed them in the innkeeper's hand. He kept his index finger on the coins pressing them down into the other man's palm. He looked him in the eyes and squinted as a surge of power went through him, through the coins and into the innkeeper.

"This is all the room is worth and is all I shall pay, do you understand me?" The innkeeper slowly nodded his head. Katrill spoke again, intensifying the power surge. The innkeeper jumped as the intensity increased.

"Now then," Katrill continued in a low subdued voice. "My friends and I would like some food, the best you have. And I do not wish the need to ask you for it again, understand me?" The innkeeper nodded his head eagerly.

"Good," Katrill said as he released him. "Bring it to us over there." He pointed to where Jodell sat.

"What kept you?" Jodell asked as he nibbled on a hard roll spread with honey.

"Oh, just getting to know the innkeeper is all," Katrill answered with a smile.

The innkeeper finally brought out some real food. There was baked white fish with wild rice, stir fried, and a huge hot bowl of seafood stew in a rich savory broth. There was also baked potatoes and thickly sliced fillet of flounder dipped in a honey and butter sauce and baked until there was a thin glaze on the top. They ate with a vengeance.

The two of them sat and sipped wine after the meal, as they waited for Orda to return. "It is time you started to learn to be a sorcerer. There are many things that one must learn before he can be truly called a sorcerer, even if he has a natural ability for it."

Katrill reached into his inside pocket and pulled out a small book of black leather. There was a serpentine head etched into the leather and overlaid in silverleaf. It was a beautiful piece of craftsmanship. The serpentine eyes were two small red rubies. He handed it to Jodell and said, "Take this book and study it."

"What is it?" Jodell asked as he reached for the small book.

"It is a book of rules as well as a book of spells. All of which must be studied and memorized. Each spell has its own set of rules as to how it should be used and when it should not be used. It is necessary that you learn this. You should know it as well as you know your name.

"The spells and rules must become second nature to you, so that you don't have to stop and think about it every time you get ready to use one. If you run across a truly competent sorcerer, your life will depend on how well you have learned. You may be a natural but there is no substitute for knowledge and experience. Remember that."

Jodell nodded in understanding and put the book in his inside jacket pocket.

Orda came in just then behind four other men. Three of them were definitely guards, the other a short fat man with a big red face and red hair. The fat man was richly dressed in silks embroidered with gold thread and trimmed in delicate lace around the hem and front. The three guards were rather short as well, though taller than their master. They wore similar gowns but of satin rather than silk and lacking the gold thread and delicate lace work. Their gowns hung nearly to their ankles with splits on either side that came up to their waist. They wore a satin sash tied around their waists which was decorated it front with a small precious stone. All four men wore their hair braided in back which also hung to their waists. The men approached the table where Jodell and Katrill sat. Orda hung back and watched.

The fat man walked over to the table, placed his fat hands on the edge and spoke, his voice commanding. "This is my table, you will both have to move immediately."

Neither of them said anything. They looked at each other for a few seconds then looked at the fat man. It was Jodell who answered him, his voice menacing.

"Go away," he said simply and resumed drinking his wine. The fat man became angry, obviously accustomed to getting his own way. He stepped back and spoke to his guards.

"Move them."

The guards started toward them. Jodell was on his feet and had his sword out in a second, only to have it kicked from his hand by the first guard. Before he could recover, a second kick hit him on the side of the head and a third, hit him in the stomach, knocking the wind out of him. He went down. Katrill also went down under a flurry of punches too fast for him to see or counter. Orda had seen this type of fighting before and knew a little of it from an old fighting instructor his father once hired to teach him and his brothers. He also knew that Jodell and Katrill didn't have much of a chance.

Orda casually walked over to where the fighting was going on and walked up behind one of the guards and buried his axe in the man's back. There was a gurgling sound as blood filled his lung, then he collapsed to the floor. A second guard had turned by then but Orda had already retrieved his axe from the first man's back.

Orda feinted a low kick, the guard dropped his hands to block and Orda reacted by swinging his axe back handed from left to right. The guard tried to evade the swing but was not fast enough. The razor sharp edge bit through his throat cleanly. Blood shot out in spurts from the severed carotids each time his heart beat. The man dropped to his knees clutching desperately at his throat, his last breath was a low rumbling like an underground stream bubbling toward the surface.

Orda turned his attention to the third guard who had just finished downing Katrill with a lightening fast kick to the abdomen. Orda knew that without the element of surprise he might not be able to defeat him. He grabbed the fat man by the neck and held him, ready to split his skull.

"Come closer and this tub of hog fat dies." The guard took another step and Orda spoke again.

"It's your decision, my friend, another step and you lose your job first, then your life, like your friends there." Orda pointed to the two lifeless corpses of the other two guards that lay in a rapidly enlarging pool of bright red blood.

Jodell had recovered and now held the point of his sword at the back of the guard's neck. The guard stood motionless for a second, then suddenly dropped, elbowed Jodell in the groin and in one smooth movement jumped to the ground and rolled into Orda, knocking him down and landing on top of him.

Three swift blows to the face and side of the head and Orda was nearly unconscious. There was a bright flash of blue-white light as Orda closed his eyes and fell into unconsciousness.

Katrill stood over the lifeless body of the third guard and the limp, unconscious form of Orda and shook his head at the waste of life. He bent down and gently rolled the charred remains of the guard off of Orda, then turned his attention to the fat man the guards had worked for, pointing his still smoking staff at the center of his fat trembling chest.

"Please, sir, spare me." The fat man begged for his life. "Please, sir, I meant you no harm, really I didn't."

"You mean us no harm!" Jodell said incredulously. "Why you fat, filthy . . ." Jodell didn't finish his sentence as he smashed his fist into the fat man's face, knocking him to the floor.

"Please, sir, don't hit me," he said as he struggled to his knees, spitting out blood from a busted lip. "You can have the table. You can have anything you want, just spare my life."

He fumbled in his jacket pocket and pulled out a small silk purse. "Here, jewels. You can have them all, but don't kill me."

The fat man pulled out five large jewels. Two blood red rubies, a smaller but perfect diamond, one sapphire and one amethyst.

"Get out of here," Katrill said. "You disgust me."

"Oh, thank you, sir, thank you. God bless you for your mercy," the fat man was saying as he made a hasty retreat out of the inn.

Katrill picked up the jewels and gave the innkeeper the amethyst. "I think this will more than pay for the damage. We will be in our room, send up some hot wine and hot water immediately. And a doctor for our friend." He and Jodell carried Orda upstairs and laid him in the bed, waiting for the doctor to arrive.

The evening turned swiftly into night and a heavy gloom settled over the city. It was a heavy preternatural gloom that was not quite a fog, but rather a heavy web of darkness that closed off the city like a black moat.

The gloom was deep and complete, yet it was somehow enticing. It settled around Jodell's eyes and ears and pressed against his temples with the gentle pressure of a feather pillow. It somehow soothed him, lulled him, causing him to relax.

The gloom pressed around his neck and wrapped itself about him in heavy swirls like coils of an efferal snake. He closed his eyes on the pressure and let it slowly caress him. His breathing slowed, his eyes fluttered and closed, his heart beat slowed. His mind was alive, however, and every inch of his nervous system was firing in rapid succession.

His body tingled with a million sensations all at once and his mind saw scenes of what he could only describe as heaven for want of a better description, for he had nothing to compare it to. He was in a world that surpassed the beauty and serenity of the fairy lands at their height of beauty and he and Jaecai were there, just the two of them laughing and talking.

He was out on the balcony of their room. There was no moon and the stars could barely be seen penetrating the heavy gloom of the winter night. Katrill was still tending Orda, who was now conscious.

Jodell was languishing in the pleasure of his daughter. She stood beside him, holding his hand and smiling up at him. Her deep black eyes sparkled with a love so deep that not even they knew the extent of it. She broke away from him and started to run, calling after him to follow her to chase her. Jodell smiled and reached out to her and started to follow her. He called out to her, calling her by name.

His calling attracted Katrill's attention, who looked up. There was a faint glow surrounding Jodell, a shimmer that throbbed and pulsed like a heart beat. Jodell had one leg over the marble rail of the balcony, still smiling and calling to Jaecai.

"Jodell, no!" Katrill screamed as he jumped up and ran for the balcony, already conjuring a spell to counter the one that held Jodell. There was a blinding flash of blue and black energy laced at the edges by a blood red energy that crackled as Katrill was attacked.

He was just barely able to deflect most of the energy, yet the force of it was still enough to knock him from his feet and throw him five feet across the room. Chunks of marble and glass and pieces of broken furniture flew back into the room like shrapnel.

Katrill lay on his back grimacing in pain but was able to protect himself and Orda. He gathered his will for an attack, he still held his staff in his hand and raised its serpentine head upright in the blackness that filled the room. He screamed out two words that Orda could not understand, two words that seemed to drift past Orda's ears rather than into them. They released a surge of power so great that the foundations of the inn trembled and every window and article of glass within a two-block radius was shattered. There was a scream, hideously bestial. It seemed to recede into the distance as the shock waves subsided. Katrill could have sworn it was a female voice, but could not be sure.

Now it was quiet again. As suddenly as it had begun, it was over. Katrill lay back on the rubble-strewn floor, a sharp pain raced through his left side and throbbed with each intake of breath. He opened his eyes and looked around for Orda and Jodell. Orda was laying on the floor beside a pile of heavy splintered wood, which had once been a bed. Jodell stood shakily in what was left of the doorway to the balcony. The balcony itself was gone and Jodell looked down from a sheer drop of ten stories at the jagged rocks below.

They had managed to survive another attack, again they had been lucky. The Hated One was becoming more clever and it was obvious that he knew about Jodell. He knew now that something had to be done. It was time for him to take some decisive action.

It was clear that Jebeialle was looking for the stones and knew that Jodell was looking for them as well, and was trying to stop him. This time his attack had been directed against

Jodell. It had been a different type of attack, more subtle and in a way, more dangerous than the first. Whoever their attacker was had wielded great power, power nearly equal to his own. That thought unnerved him. If Jebeialle had the help and loyalty of adepts, this mission would be a hard one indeed.

Katrill lay for a while with his eyes closed, feeling the residual energies that still gyrated in the now quiet room. There was something familiar about it. He recognized the feeling of that energy but the sensations were weak and nondescript. There was also something different about it. He felt a type of familiarity that he could not describe. The sensations were diminishing more and more and he pushed it to the back of his mind.

Jodell walked over to him and knelt down. His grey flecked eyes seemed greyer, older somehow. "Are you hurt, old man?" Jodell asked.

"I'll be fine, just a couple of busted ribs, I think, and a lot of bruises." Katrill grimaced as a pain shot through his left side. "I shall need your help, my friend, I am not strong enough to repair myself."

Jodell nodded his agreement. "Give me your right hand." Katrill took Jodell's hand and placed the tips of his fingers on his forehead and had him place his left hand on his chest over the broken ribs.

"Now, my friend, relax, let your mind go and allow me to enter. That's it, more, more, relax and let me do all the work."

Jodell sat beside the sleeping Katrill as if to keep watch over him. He had grown exceedingly fond of this old man who had twice now saved his life and nearly lost his own in doing so. He had come to respect this old man in a way he had never respected anyone before.

He sat and looked down into Katrill's time etched face and saw the lines of pain there. He suddenly felt ashamed of the way he had treated him. He had gone so far as to threaten him. He had been selfish, thinking only of himself while the old man was thinking of the world, which included him.

Jodell looked down at Katrill and spoke to him. "I am sorry, old man, for all the sorrow and grief I have caused you. But I have been through so much in the last few years, much more than any man should have to go through. I had begun to think that I was the only one in the world with problems. I had come to believe that my needs were beyond any others and I am sorry for that. You taught me that I was wrong and I respect you for that. I guess I've been alone for too long, kept to myself, hidden away from others even from myself, but you woke me up to a greater need than my own and I appreciate that."

Katrill moved and groaned a little but did not wake. The expression on his face, however, had changed and he looked a bit more comfortable.

Orda watched the two of them from the other side of the room but didn't disturb them. He cleared a spot on the rubble strewn floor, stretched out his blanket and lay down to sleep for the remainder of the night.

The next day found the three of them packing. Katrill was still badly shaken. His side still throbbed a bit but that would soon pass and he would be good as new. All he needed was rest. But he knew that he could not afford to rest. His mission was becoming urgent and he had to move.

He heard reports of attacks on outlying villages where everyone was slaughtered and knew Jebeialle was stepping up the war. Slowly he was escalating the fighting. Already the northernmost provinces of Sartoe were fighting a border war with the trolls trying to keep them in check, but there were too many of them and small raiding parties were slipping through.

The Sartorian army was small and weak, a vestige of what it once was. Reports were coming in of a massive army of trolls led by ogres moving slowly across the northern wastes.

They were being hampered by the snow but were making their way slowly south. It was but a matter of time before they reached the border of Sartoe, then the war would begin in earnest.

Katrill knew the only way to stop the ensuing bloodshed was to kill the ogre king and throw their army into confusion. He had to go to he Valley of Shadows. Jebeialle would probably not make it out alive. There was one place he had to go first and he might not get the chance again. He had to go see Mother once more.

Katrill was sitting on his horse enamored in thought while Jodell and Orda took care of paying their bill, which turned out to be sizeable because of the damage from the previous night. Katrill's mind raced as he thought about what was transpiring in the world. He felt himself to blame for it. If he had only shown Jebeialle more friendship, more compassion those many years ago, if he had been there when his friend needed him most, perhaps the world would not be in the crisis it was in.

He had begun to blame himself more and more as time progressed. His pride and ambition had kept him from being a true friend. He had been full of pride and felt himself above all others because he had been a gifted student and had surpassed most of the other students, novices and upperclassmen alike. He had been good, really good, so good that he had gotten the position that Jebeialle had sought and was expected to get even before he had come to the order. That had been the final insult. Jebeialle could not take it, he had revolted and as a result, left the order vowing to get even with everyone.

Katrill brought his hands up to his face and rubbed his eyes until they blurred. His head was spinning, he was falling into the pit of his own fears. He was falling into a deep depression because he felt to blame for everything that happened to Jebeialle. He was to blame for what had happened to Jodell and his daughter. He was to blame for what happened to Orda's people and for what was happening to others at that very moment.

He felt he was to blame for more details than he could count. The blood of thousands lay spilled upon the ground and it called out to him for vengeance. He had been responsible for their deaths and the only way they could rest was for him to die.

Images of people danced before his eyes, pointing accusing fingers at him, poking at his heart until he could not take it any longer. He was sitting on his horse, rubbing his eyes and shaking uncontrollably. His horse was becoming agitated and threatened to bolt. Orda was holding his reins calling his name, fighting the bucking horse. Jodell came over and helped quiet the horse. He reached up and grabbed Katrill and nearly screamed. A surge of power went through him cutting into his body like a knife.

Katrill's eyes were red with anger and a blue shimmer encapsulated his face and hands. "Don't touch me," he shouted, pointing a threatening finger at Jodell.

"Katrill, what's wrong with you, what has happened?" Jodell asked as he picked himself up from the ground.

"What isn't wrong," Katrill screamed back. There was a bright flash of blue-white light that lit the morning up like a super nova. In an instant Katrill was gone. All that was left was a faint shimmer of an outline where he had been. Jodell was the only one able to see it.

Orda rubbed at his light blinded eyes. "What the hell happened?"

"I'm not sure," answered Jodell. "But I think we had better hurry up and get to the Valley of Shadows." They mounted their horses and rode out of town. Jodell felt a chill at his back, like something had touched his spine while probing for his heart. But the feeling didn't last long so he ignored it and rode on.

Nine

Katrill appeared on the desert plains of Tithe. The sands lay out before him like a vast endless frozen sea. It was hot, insanely hot, and Katrill started sweating almost as soon as he appeared. The sandy sea was vast and open except for six purposely placed boulders placed one beside the other in a huge semicircle. To most people they had lost their meaning, but Katrill knew. They marked the point of passage to the City of Leaves.

The stones formed a semicircle that faced inward toward the south, toward the outstretched sea of endless white sand. Katrill rode into the semicircle pressing his right palm to the center stone. At first nothing happened, then there was a slight whining sound like little children crying. Then it grew in pitch and turned to a loud hum. The sound was different now, it sounded like a chorus of sweet-sounding voices, humming softly.

Katrill didn't allow himself to listen to it. It was a beautiful song but he knew it to be a beautiful trap for the unwary and uninvited. He remembered how he had nearly been trapped by it the first time he came to visit Mother. He had heard the song and was fascinated by it. It sounded as if it came directly from the stone. He approached it, examining it and was nearly pulled into the stone itself. He had been lucky that day and managed to escape. Many had not.

There was a surge of power and he vanished. When he reappeared, he stood on what appeared to be huge leaves.

They lay overlapping each other and formed a vast landscape as far as he could see. Branches and trunks of trees rose up from beneath the leaves, rising hundreds of feet into the air above him. There were spaces between the leaves here and there where he could see down. He was standing high up in what appeared to be huge trees ten thousand or more feet tall. Some of the trunks were hollowed out to form living spaces. He could hear noises like people moving about, but saw no one. He had been here before, a number of times but he had never seen the people.

He looked up to where the tallest tree had been hollowed out at its very top. A dome was formed over the opening by more of the huge leaves. He could see the entrance through a gap in the leaves. It was dark and quiet. It was here he wanted to go. It was the home of Mother.

He started walking and stopped, a silvery gray shimmer flashed at the side of his eyes then quickly disappeared. There was a deep rumbling sound like distant thunder rolling in the hills. He reacted instinctively. His staff flared bright blue as he brought it up in front of him, just as the first bolt struck. The fire crackled and shimmered, sparks flew and fell to the ground leaving dark scorched patches on the leaves, as the bolt shattered into a million dark red and purple fragments.

The second bolt came immediately behind the first with greater power behind it. Katrill was knocked backwards as he deflected it. A third bolt was already hurtling toward him as he regained his balance. He pointed his staff, his lips moving swiftly, uttering some long lost language. A power surge of power exploded from the head of his staff. Blue-white energy leaped through the air. It met the blood red energy in mid-air and exploded with a sound that caused the entire city to shake. It shattered the bolt of energy directed at him and continued on toward its target. It struck his attacker in the center of his chest. Katrill didn't wait to see if it had been effective. He moved forward, his eyes squinted, his teeth clenched as his words flowed across his lips and his free hand made an arcane symbol in the air.

Another burst of power followed the first, this one more intense. It struck his attacker in the abdomen, exploding into his gut. Fragments of flesh and a shower of blood sprinklets fell everywhere, painting the leafy ground a brilliant red.

Katrill stared at the twisted heap of smoldering flesh, his eyes red, sweat beading on his forehead from the exertion. He spun around as a deep harsh voice spoke to him from behind, cutting at his already raw nerves.

"Very well done, Katrill. Very well done, indeed. I don't think I could have done better myself," the man said.

He was a tall thin man. His hair was long and brown and fell across his face nearly hiding it. His gown was white, trimmed in red, and tied at the waist with a red silk sash. He also carried a long staff but his terminated with the head of a boar, its white ivory tusks gleaming in the bright sunlight.

"Who are you?" Katrill demanded, as he placed his staff directly before him at eye level.

"You mean you have forgotten me already? My, my, you are getting old aren't you?" He scoffed at Katrill trying to provoke him.

"Come on, old man, think. Think hard. I'm sure it'll come back to you."

"Ribshondra," Katrill said as the other man's voice registered in his memory.

"So, you do remember. That's good, old man. I want you to remember me. Remember that it was you who had me expelled from the academy. You told on me."

"You were doing wrong, it was my duty. I tried to reason with you but you would not listen."

"Your duty!" Ribshondra spat in fury. "It was none of your business." He quickly regained his composure as he smiled at Katrill wickedly.

"It doesn't matter now, though. I never forgave you for that. I'm going to make you pay for that." Katrill lifted his staff preparing to defend himself.

The other man backed off a little, raising his hands to where they could be seen. "Now, don't get excited, old man. I won't fight you here. I don't think Mother would appreciate that. You know how easily upset she is." He was smiling all the while he talked.

"Too bad that one didn't know that." He looked at the remains of Katrill's attacker, which still smoldered. "You know he was a pupil of mine, very talented, like yourself. He had a very promising future ahead of him. Oh, well, so much for that. I was never very good at teaching anyway."

Katrill turned and started walking away. "Old man," Ribshondra called after him. "I won't fight you here. But I'll be waiting for you on the other side."

Katrill continued walking without looking back. He heard the thin, whining sound and then the smooth humming of what sounded like voices as the other man was transported away.

He walked slowly toward Mother's tree, he felt sick. He could still smell the charred flesh of the man he had just killed. He had been so young, so stupid. He thought that there had been no need to kill him. Here in the City of Leaves, if one sorcerer attacked another, Mother would intervene and discipline him. But he had reacted too quickly and had not stopped to think.

He shook his head as he stopped at the base of Mother's tree, looking up to where the entrance was. He should not be blaming himself. He had a right to defend himself, even here. He should not feel responsible for everything that happened. This boy had been working for Jebeialle and he was responsible for Jebeialle.

He closed his eyes then concentrated on feeling mother's presence. He found it. It seemed to come from everywhere. The trees, the leaves, even the air was alive with her presence. He spoke to her.

"I seek permission to enter."

"You may enter, my son," Mother answered him, her voice soft and soothing, almost alluring.

"Thank you, Mother," he said. He spread his hands out to both sides, palms downward and levitated himself up to the opening.

At first he hesitated. The darkness was foreboding. It seeped out of the hollowed out trunk and washed up against the sides as it dispersed in the bright sunlight. He tentatively put his hand forward, testing the air. There was no reason for him to be afraid, not really. This was the home of Mother. Nothing would happen to him here, she would not allow it. Not even Jebeialle would attack him here. This was neutral ground, protected by mother and her authority came directly from the gods.

Still, he was a sorcerer, trained to be careful. He tested the air, felt for anything out of the ordinary. He found nothing. Then he started to move forward into the entrance.

"Leave your staff." Mother's voice was inside his head clear and strong. He started to protest.

"Leave it, you will not need it here," she explained. He laid it beside the opening, hesitating to release it.

"Do not be concerned. It will be there when you return." Her voice filled his head, so that his own thoughts were pushed aside. He could think of nothing but what she was saying when she spoke.

When she stopped talking, the silence in his mind was poignant. It took an effort to fight down the hollow emptiness her voice left behind and fill it with his own thoughts.

It had been a long time since he last visited her. He had missed her gravely. He missed the soothing pressure of her voice as it rolled across her lips and bathed his mind with its vibrations. Her voice lulled him, made him want to sleep. He was like a little boy who had done something wrong and now had to face his parents and account for it. He knew they would not hurt him, would probably forgive him. Yet, he was afraid just the same because he had not come back to see her sooner.

He stood just outside the entrance peering into the absolute dark, steeling his nerves. He wondered what Jodell and Orda were doing, he hoped they were okay. He knew they were probably worried about him and knew they would try and follow him. But he had the advantage. It would take them a week at least to get to the Valley of Shadows and ogres' pit, but by then his job would be finished.

He took a few deep breaths and readied himself. He knew he would be tested by mother and he wanted to be ready. He closed his eyes for a few seconds, adjusting them to darkness, found the opening with his hands and stepped into the pitch blackness. He stopped. There was no movement, no sound. He called to her.

"Mother!" There was no answer. He called again.

"Mother!" He waited, started to call a third time when a faint flicker of light caught his eye. It glowed almost imperceptibly for a moment, then died.

"I am here," came the soft musical voice of the woman he knew only as Mother. "Come to me."

"I need to talk to you," Katrill said almost to himself. If anyone had been standing beside him, they would not have heard him.

"Come to me," she repeated. "We will talk."

"How will I find you?" Katrill asked. He still had not moved.

"Follow the flame." Again, the flame flickered, a pinpoint of light lost in a sea of black. He spotted it, locked in on it, and started moving forward. He moved forward slowly, carefully, feeling the ground with his mind like a blind man feels it with a stick.

He stopped. There was a pit directly in front of him. He could hear water as it gushed and gurgled deep within the pit. He could smell it, fresh and clean. Suddenly he was thirsty, desperately thirsty. He bent toward the hole, then stopped, caught himself. He resisted, pushed the thought from his mind and stepped around the pit.

"Mother," he called again. "Where are you?"

"Where are you?" Her voice came back, calm, soothing.

"Mother, please. I must talk to you," he pleaded.

"Come to me," she said again. He moved on slowly, deliberately. He moved one foot then the other. He stopped again, listening. He swept the area with his mind, nothing. He took another step then jumped back. He heard the buzzing first, like the sound a mosquito makes at night when it buzzes in one's ear. He felt the wind, caught it, pulled it back. It was an arrow. He turned it over in his hands, then it vanished. He moved on. He walked slowly in the darkness, his eyes shut, seeing with his mind.

Again came the flame. It flickered, nearly died and then began to grow. Soon it was a raging fire. He could feel the heat as it grew and moved toward him. He didn't move. It stopped before him and began to swirl and take on a shape. Soon it had taken on the shape of a person, a little boy about twelve. He stood before Katrill, a peevish little smile on his face. He had one tooth missing in the front. He also had a dagger in his hand.

"Fight him," her voice commanded.

"No," he said. "I cannot."

"Fight him!" she repeated.

"No."

"Then you must leave."

"I must talk to you, Mother, please!"

"Use your dagger," she said. Katrill drew his dagger. The boy circled him, a foolish grin on his face. He charged. Katrill raised his dagger, side stepped and brought the handle of his dagger down on the side of the boy's head. His hand passed through him. The boy turned and smiled at him again, then vanished.

The flame came once more. He locked onto it with his mind, held it. It tried to die but he would not let it. It began to grow. It became a soft spotlight with no apparent source. It shone on a soft red pillow.

"You are welcome, my son," her voice said in its usual musical pitch.

Katrill sat down on the pillow. Only then did she appear before him. She was an old lady but at the same time, very young. Her features were very fine yet blunt at the same time. She was beautiful but also extremely homely. She was anything and everything he wanted her to be. She was everything to everyone, therefore, nothing to anyone. She was simply who she was—she was Mother.

"Why do you test me, Mother?" Katrill asked.

"You know the rules," she said.

"But you make the rules."

"Yes, I do."

"Is it really necessary?" he asked.

"Yes," she said simply. He signed deeply, steepling his fingers in thought.

"Are you well?" she asked.

"Yes, I'm fine."

"Are you sure?"

"Yes."

"You wanted to talk to me?" she asked.

"Yes." Still he did not speak up. He stared at his hands.

"Are you sure you are well? What troubles you?"

"Yes," he said again. "I'm just tired."

"Of what?"

"Everything. The entire business," he said.

"You are too young to be tired," she said. "How old are you?"

"Two thousand years."

"Do you know my age?"

"No."

"Guess."

"I cannot."

"Try."

"Five thousand?" he guessed.

"Ten thousand?" She smiled at him, knowingly.

"I was old when the world was created. So do not speak to me of tired. I am tired. You are but a child." They sat across from each other for long moments without speaking.

"Who is she?" she asked pointedly.

"She is a pleasant woman from a small village in northern most Sartoe," he said.

"You know it is forbidden. A sorcerer must stay celibate."

"Yes . . . I mean no. We cannot marry. The rule doesn't say we must stay celibate."

"Then it should. Look where it has gotten you."

"Yes," he agreed.

"What will you do?" she asked.

"What can I do?"

"Nothing," she said matter of factly.

"Mother."

"Yes."

"We need your help."

"We!"

"Jodell and I."

"Have I met him yet?"

"No. He isn't ready."

"What can I do?"

"Tell us where to find the power Stones of the Elves."

"I cannot."

"Why not?" he asked.

"Because it isn't allowed."

"Why not?"

"I don't know. I didn't make that rule."

"Who then?" he asked.

"The gods, I suppose."

"Is there no chance?" he asked her.

"No." Katrill threw up his hands in exasperation.

"It's just as well though," she said. "If I tell you I have to tell him. He was here you know."

"Who?" Katrill asked, half listening.

"Jebeialle."

"He came to see you and you let him in?" Katrill asked angrily.

"Has the right. He passed the test," she said. Her voice was still calm, soothing. It soothed Katrill until his anger was drained from him.

"I did not make that rule either. I cannot take sides."

"Then my trip here was for nothing," Katrill's voice sounded hopeless.

"I have missed you, you know. It has been a long time since you were here, her voice changed. It sounded suddenly older, weaker. He realized he had wounded her, for she truly loved him like a mother.

"I'm sorry, Mother, I'm so very tired. I didn't mean that. It was worth the trip and the test to see you again." He was sincere. She beamed at him happily. Her love for him showing clearly in her old-young eyes.

"Mother."

"Yes, my son."

"Can you tell me what is there for me. I mean, will I see you again?"

"No," she said.

"Then my time is near?" he asked.

"Yes."

"Thank you, Mother. I must go now. There isn't much time left." He got up and walked to the entrance. She called him before he left.

"My son." He turned and looked into her saddened eyes.

"Yes, Mother." She walked over to him, embraced him for a long time in silence, kissed him on the lips, then released him.

"The elves were entrusted by the gods as the keepers of the stones. They hid them in the golden pommel of a sword."

"Thank you, mother," he said. He stood and looked at her with tear-filled eyes. There were so many things he wanted to say to her, so many things he wanted to share with her. But he didn't know where to begin, how to start. He could only look at her with longing in his eyes. She smiled at him with understanding.

"I know, my son. I know."

"I love you, Mother," was all he said. He turned and left without looking back. She didn't say anything for a long time. Finally she spoke, but he couldn't hear her this time.

"Goodbye, my son, and sleep well." Then she began to cry.

The sun still hung high overhead, heating the air almost beyond endurance. The air was stifling after the cool dampness of mother's place. Katrill didn't think about what had just transpired between him and mother, didn't allow himself to. He couldn't afford the emotional implications of what she had just said. He knew he would not survive his encounter with

Jebeialle, but that didn't matter. He felt responsible for him anyway, so it was natural that he had to pay for what he caused.

The thing that caused the most pain was that he would never see Mother again. I was not that he would miss her, he would be dead, unable to feel the pain of their separation. He felt for mother. He knew how much she loved him and knew she would suffer from his death. She would be aware of it at the instant of his death, and he would not be able to do anything about it. There wouldn't be anyone to console her the way she had consoled him so many times before.

He stopped, turned and looked back at the dark entrance to her home. He thought he heard the soft sound of weeping but couldn't be sure. The sound eluded him and was gone. He turned and walked out of the sunlight into the shade of a huge leaf and disappeared.

Ribshondra was waiting for him on the other side as he had promised. Katrill had forgotten about him and was preparing to ride on when the taller man called to him. He was standing atop the huge stones silhouetted against the desert sun. His white gown blew behind him from a gentle but steady breeze.

"I told you I would be waiting for you, old man." His tone was deadly. "I will not be cheated out of the pleasure of killing you."

Katrill let out a sigh of resignation. "Come down then. It would not be wise to risk damaging Mother's stones."

Ribshondra levitated himself down. He stared at Katrill, his staff already glowing a deep ruby red, which was nearly undiscernable in the bright sunlight. Katrill started walking around him, trying to maneuver him into position. He wanted the sun to be in Ribshondra's eyes. He talked to him as he walked, distracting him, taking his mind off of what he was doing.

"I see your abilities have improved, or is it Jebeaille's power that you wield?"

"I do not need anyone else to defeat you. I am stronger than you."

"You think so?" Katrill said as he continued circling until he was in the position he wanted to be in. He was standing between Ribshondra and the stones. Ribshondra was facing the sun, squinting his eyes against the glare.

"It'll take more than just raw power to defeat me. It'll take a lot of experience as well as skill to defeat me," Katrill said. "You're more stupid than I thought you were if you think you can kill me. You are not my match. You are not ready for a master, and you are a fool if you think you will leave here alive." Ribshondra's eyes blazed in fury.

"Oh, I'll leave here alive alright. The only one who will die today is you old man." Ribshondra raised his hands over his head and began a low chant. A dark purple-black cloud began to form over his head, crackling with power. Katrill threw a bolt of bright blue energy which struck the center of Ribshondra's chest, knocking him off his feet.

"Get up and fight me," Katrill said mockingly. "You're too slow. You'll never get me like that. Get up and try it again." Ribshondra began gathering his will again, but Katrill struck him again, knocking him down again.

"Come on, get up. Let's play some more," Katrill was saying as he struck him with a third bolt.

Ribshondra stood up screaming with rage. He gathered his will and threw a powerful bolt of black-red energy at Katrill. Katrill was waiting for this. He dropped to the ground, allowing the bolt to pass over his head. The bolt struck the stones. They responded immediately. They began to vibrate and hum, louder and louder. Katrill and Ribshondra had to hold their ears against the sound.

The stones began to glow first red then blue, until they appeared white hot. Suddenly the hum stopped and a brilliant white beam shot from the stones and struck Ribshondra. He screamed as the beam wrapped itself around him like a cocoon and began pulling him toward the stones.

"Help me, Katrill, please help me. I don't want to die like this, not this way," Ribshondra screamed as he struggled against the cocoon. Katrill could see flashes of red from inside the cocoon where Ribshondra fought to get out.

"Please, Katrill, help me," he pleaded as he was slowly drawn into the stone.

"You will not die, Ribshondra," Katrill said. "You will live forever."

"Please, please, help me. Katrill pleasseee . . ." Ribshondra's voice trailed off as he was drawn fully into the stone.

Soon the desert was quiet again. Only the wind spoke now. It had picked up a bit and was blowing sand against Katrill's back. He stood up and watched the now quiescent stones for a while. He could almost see Ribshondra's face in the sand-smoothed surface of the stone.

It was getting late, the air was beginning to cool. The sun had nearly dropped completely below the horizon. Katrill remounted his horse, turned and started away from the stones. His body and his horse shimmered and began to fade out slowly as they rode, until they were gone.

Ten

The sky was a brilliant hue of dusty rose and lent the landscape an almost artificial texture. The land looked animated like a giant cartoon superimposed upon the horizon. If not for the gaping maw of the ogres' pit, the landscape would have been a paradise.

The land itself was laid out in a series of rolling hills, low grass covered mounds that glistened in the waning sunlight as it reflected from the dew-covered blades. In the distance were several varieties of trees that eventually led to the southern forest ranges, leagues to the south and finally to the swamplands.

The air was alive with activity. Birds flew overhead, swooping in and out of the tall grasses singing joyfully, for here it was eternally summer. They appeared to put on a show as they displayed their aerial prowess. Here Katrill could have been content to live his life out as a normal human, free of the strictures and responsibilities of a sorcerer. Here he could lay bare his soul to the elements until they cleansed him of all guilt that was tied up in his existence.

Here he could have been free to forget the rest of the world, live his life from day to day and truly live, something he had not done for a long time. He sampled what life could be like in that small Sartorian village with Cassie and her mother. He wanted that life now. They had shown him a new aspect of life, a new dimension of living and he missed that now.

He was afraid to leave the life he had known for so long. His clan was all he had known since his mother died when he was a teenager. His relationship with the clan had always been strong and he had never questioned his role in it before. It was his life, a life he had chosen and had come to love. The thought of turning his back on a lifetime cut deeply into his sense of security, yet he was obviously displeased with his lot in life. It was affecting his judgment. Something had to be done and there was no one who could do it but him. He gathered his resolve about himself and spurred his horse forward, slowly and cautiously.

Ogres' pit was the entrance to what was known as the Valley of Shadows. It was a huge pit perhaps four to five hundred feet across. One edge of it angled in and sloped down into the ground. Inside the sloped ground spiraled downward for another seven or eight hundred feet; the pit was cast in total darkness. Katrill stopped.

The blackness was absolute. He could feel it pressing against him. It made the hair on his neck move as he stood silent, allowing his eyes to adjust to the darkness. They never did. He had experienced blackness like this before during that battle only a few days before with one of the Hated One's servants. This blackness was unnatural like the vile power that had been hurled at him, thick and omni-present.

He steeled his nerves and continued on. He felt the blackness brushing, rubbing at his face and body like a million tiny fingers, feeling every detail of his body. He stopped as he realized what this was. This was not only a means of discouraging visitors but a means of identifying them and warning the inhabitants of their presence. He had not expected this or he would have concealed himself, but now it was too late for that so he moved on, slowly but steadily.

Finally the slope began to level out, he was nearing the bottom of the pit. Katrill took another step and stopped, there were noises ahead. He could just barely make them out, soft rustling sounds of fur against rock. He stood still and listened, his mind controlled his horse and at the same time reached out ahead of him. He could not physically see in the darkness but he was a master sorcerer and there were other ways of seeing than with eyes.

He shut his eyes and concentrated. Slowly the thick blackness began to part. It moved away from his line of sight in thick swirls, never completely lifting but clearing adequately enough so that he could make out images. There was someone ahead, hidden among the shadowed corners of the caverns. He counted four of them. Three ogres and one human or nearly so. They knew he was here, they waited for him. The near human radiated an aura, he was a minor magician of no consequence, sent to slow him or maybe distract him until the ogres could kill him.

"It will not be that easy I'm afraid," Katrill spoke aloud, as he mentally commanded his horse to stay and he himself walked forward and rounded the final curve to where they waited.

*　　*　　*

The afternoon sky was a huge blue jewel that sparkled across the landscape laying down deep dark shadows from clouds that scuttled across its face. The day was clean and clear, but still cold. There was no wind to speak of, just an occasional breath of air that jostled Jodell's hair on his neck. He and Orda rode in single file heading south for the Valley of Shadows, which was a full three-days' ride, six if they stopped to rest at night.

They had left Dalmouth hours ago yet Jodell could not get it out of his mind. There was something wrong, something grating at his nerves that he could not pinpoint. He felt uneasy as if his nerves were coming unraveled. He found himself looking back to assure himself that Orda was still there. Jodell took a deep breath to try to relax, he was feeling unusually nervous, unusually anxious.

He brought his hand up to his forehead and wiped away a drop of perspiration that threatened to roll down into his eyes. His heart was beating a little faster than it should have and all his muscles were taut. He tried to will himself to relax, told himself he was tired, needed rest, told himself that it would soon pass. He rode in silence, his eyes darting from side to side at every little noise, his back straight with anticipation and trepidation.

He struggled with himself throughout the rest of the day and into the early night. They finally camped near dawn, ate a hastily prepared meal and lay down to try and catch a few hours sleep. Orda fell asleep as soon as his head hit the ground. For Jodell, sleep was a long time coming. He lay on his back and eyed the star-filled sky. His eyes danced in his head like the flame from their fire danced on the twigs that fed it.

Jodell finally fell into sleep, but it too was haunted by fear. All his childhood fears came back to him in a rush. He was a little boy of only six years of age. He lay in a huge bed in the dark, the covers drawn up over his head, huddled in a ball. The wind was blowing, shutters banging against the house. The wind whistled through the trees like the call of the dead and spoke only to him. Lightening flashed and great claps of thunder shook the house. He wanted to go to his mother but was afraid to come from under the cover so he lay there, a tiny ball of infantile fear, and cried.

Then he was in the forest beneath the towering oaks, sent to collect wild berries. The forest was quiet and dark and he was afraid. Eyes glowed in the darkness from the bushes, watched him from everywhere. A leaf fell from above somewhere and brushed his arm. He screamed and ran, tripped over a root and fell. Something moved and scampered from beneath him from the underbrush, and he screamed again. He called his mother but she could not hear him, couldn't help him. The forest was dark and lonely and large. He was afraid, afraid to run and afraid to stay where he was so he screamed and screamed until he was hoarse—until no more tears came.

Then he was older, seventeen. He sat in a dimly lighted room, lit with rush lights. The room was filled with the scent of hyacinth and honeyscukle and the air was thick with it and made his stomach turn. He closed his eyes and fought down the urge to vomit. There were others in the room, he could hear voices, low hushed voices, the kind that kept secrets. But he didn't want to know their secret. He was sitting with his back to them with his elbows propped on his knees and his face cupped between his hands.

He was crying and he didn't know why. He wiped a tear from his cheek and looked at it. It reflected the dull yellow of the rush lights back at him like a yellowed diamond sparkling dimly. He did not look back at the people behind him, they did not concern him, they with their secrets, he was beyond that. All he wanted to do was cry. He didn't know why but it was enough that he wanted to, so he did.

Then he was suddenly alone. He became suddenly aware of the silence, hollow with an echo that he felt rather than heard. An echo that said, "Turn around and face me for the last time."

He felt suddenly afraid. He was alone and did not want to be. He was not just alone in the room, he was alone in the world and was suddenly afraid that he would not survive. His heart began to pound and more tears came. The echo pulled at him, spoke to him. "Turn and face me for the last time."

He stood and turned around and his heart seemed to stop. All his blood rushed to his head until he felt faint. In the far corner was a box of plain birch. A candle burned atop it, keeping a solitary vigil like the last light of an extinguished soul. He walked toward the box, though he didn't know he had and laid his hands on top of it. He felt a surge of something like a pulse of heat as a shiver ran through him. He jerked away.

His heart throbbed like that of a frightened kitten. He wanted to run and hide somewhere and cry. But that echo came again, clear and insistent. "Face me for the last time." He pulled the top back and stood for a second, transfixed. Nothing registered in his mind. He brushed aside a stray lock of his mother's hair, bent over and kissed her firmly on the lips then collapsed to the floor and screamed.

Jodell bolted upright in his bedroom, his heart beating frantically in his ears. His eyes were blurred with fright induced tears and his hands gripped his blanket for dear life. He sat up breathing hard. The harder he tried to control his heart the faster his heart beat until it was racing wildly. He grabbed at his chest. The pain that radiated from his heart into his arms and head spread down into his torso, building pressure with each passing second. He slumped back into his pallet, his skin ashen as the pain intensified. He let out a groan like the growl of a frightened dog.

Orda was awakened by the commotion and was staring at him not knowing what to do. Jodell was fast losing consciousness, soon it would be over, he would have peace and the Hated One would have won. But he didn't care, his wife was gone, his daughter was gone. Nothing mattered anymore, not life, his nor anyone else's. He told Katrill, "I have a right." But what right did he really have, what right did anyone have to anything? The only thing he had a right to was death. But somehow that death didn't seem right, it was not time for him to die, at least not this way. He had not been able to choose his own happiness in life, he had been cheated of that. He would not be cheated of choosing his own death.

112

He was at the brink, floundering, but he would not let go. Slowly he gathered his will and began to push back the blackness that gathered around him and squeezed at his heart. At first it resisted but then it began to part and receded under his will until he was able to open his eyes. He screamed his protest at the attempt to take him. He shouted angrily as he bolted upright. "No!"

The flames of the campfire came to life, flared and shot toward him. He felt the heat, intense and unnatural. It engulfed him, wrapped itself around him like a flaming blanket. He could smell the hatred, feel the evil of the fire as it tried to consume him.

But he was not ready to die. His anger erupted like a geyser. Twin beams of power erupted from his eyes and met the flames. The night turned to day from the brilliance of the clash. For one instant, everything seemed to stand still, then the flames shattered like glass and fell away in sputtering fragments, hissing and dying as they hit the damp ground.

It was over. Jodell tottered on his feet, power oozing from the corner of his eyes, like flaming blood. His arms flayed as he started to fall. Orda caught him and helped him to a sitting position. Orda spoke to him to calm him. "It's alright now, it's over. You won."

Jodell grasped Orda's hand and squeezed it. "Did you see it? Did I kill it? Are we safe yet?" Orda looked at Jodell in dismay. His eyes were blistering around the rims and swollen completely closed. His face was red and his skin peeled. His hair was singed and his clothing burned nearly completely off.

"It's over now, you killed it. Whatever it was is gone now." Jodell lay back on his blanket, his breathing fast but regular.

"Good! Good!" He lay back and immediately passed out into merciful unconsciousness.

Jodell slept quietly all the next day. Orda woke him periodically to make him drink some medicine he had distilled from some wild varieties of dried herbs he carried in his saddle pouch. Jodell was recovering rapidly. His breathing had become normal again during the night and by morning most of the swelling of his eyes had receded and his color was returning. Orda treated his blistering eyes with a poultice made from mashed, boiled leaves and already, they were showing signs of healing. By mid afternoon, Jodell was coherent though still exhausted to the point of totality. Yet his strength was returning rapidly and his appetite growing. By late evening, the blisters were almost gone and only a slight darkening of the skin betrayed that anything had been wrong.

Jodell awoke during the night to eat and talk a little, but he would quickly fall back into deep sleep, sometimes while talking. They made their camp there and remained for three days, waiting for Jodell to recover. At the end of the third day, Jodell was ready to travel. Though he was not fully recovered, he did not want to lose any more time, he had to get moving.

On the fourth day they started out again, leaving behind a burned out patch of ground where they had camped. They started early before the sunrise. The morning was cold and offensive. It permeated their heavy hides until they felt they may as well have nothing on, but they endured, they had no choice. Jodell slept in his saddle while Orda led his horse. He was still very weak and easily succumbed to the lulling of the cold to close his eyes and sleep.

His dreams were not undisturbed. Visions of past fears still haunted him. Residual effects of his battle, a grim reminder of the power he was up against. He had won that battle only because he was determined to plot his own future but he had nearly died, nearly giving into the temptation of death.

The attack at Dalmouth had been similar and he had nearly fallen for the same tactic and this time he hadn't had Katrill to pull him through. But he had prevailed this time.

The poignancy of the fact struck him deeply. "This time. This time." He repeated it to himself over and over. Katrill had told him, "There is no substitute for knowledge and experience. Your life may depend on it." Well, he was certainly getting the experience, all he lacked was the knowledge.

He reached into his saddle bag and pulled out the small book Katrill had given him and began reading it. Next time he did not want to be found wanting.

They stopped at a small outland farm late that evening and bought some dried beef from its owner. They made camp on the outskirts of a small town late that night. They didn't enter town, didn't want to chance running into any trouble. The night was bitter cold and the wind blew in from the north bringing with it the bitter cold of the mountain air.

They made camp beside a low hillock that afforded little protection from the wind and built a small fire, just enough to warm some wine. They didn't want to chance a large fire that might attract attention. The night passed uneventfully but slowly. Jodell was too cold to sleep. He stayed up all night reading and memorizing. Orda managed a few quick naps, but could not sleep well, the cold air constantly woke him. By morning they were chilled to the bone and moved about stiffly, as they packed their blankets to move on.

About midday the sun came out and the day warmed considerably. The blood returned to Jodell's feet and hands until he could feel them again. Pins seemed to stick in his feet and hands as sensation returned. They passed the town without incident, riding steadily south and slightly west. It began to snow late, lightly at first and then became heavier as night approached. By nightfall it was coming down in a thick blanket of pure white crystals.

The moon was out but was hiding behind snow-filled clouds so that the night was unusually dark. The snow was peaceful looking, falling quietly upon the ground. The snow was light and flakey and radiated peacefulness. Jodell stretched his canvas tent over them, it made an adequate shelter against the snow. He sat and watched it fall, a flake at a time, slowly piling up a uniform layer of whiteness.

Late the next day they crossed the huge flat plains of the middle kingdoms and came to the upper reaches of the Aldmerian Highlands. They were huge humps of rolling earth, just short of being mountains. The ascent up into the highlands was slow for they were at the dividing line between the cold wintry countries and the warmer temperate countries and the snows were already beginning to melt. The hills were huge mounds of thick mud and slush that splattered the legs of both Jodell and Orda. In places the mud came up nearly to the sides of the horses but these areas were rare and would have been dust pits in the summer.

Once in the hills the land spread out before them like crumpled paper. Here and there were scattered trees throughout the landscape, huge boulders jutted out of the ground like the cracked teeth of the lower jaw of some huge beast left to dry rot in the damp cool air. To the west a few hundred yards was a small waterfall that swept over a boulder and wore it thin as water gurgled up from the depths of the hills. It flowed through a small channel cut into the rock after hundreds of years and finally disappeared into the ground, soaked up like a giant dirt sponge. Here crabs and small game flourished for the underground water was fresh. Here vegetables were plentiful and the lush greenery made the land come alive. Jodell and Orda stopped here to rest their horses and themselves.

Jodell's mind still churned from the previous day and his mind raced with fear for Katrill. He was afraid that something would happen to him, and he felt at fault. He should have been able to help him, should have recognized that something was wrong and tried to do something. He once said that he owed the world nothing, but now he felt responsibility for every man, woman, and child on earth—not because he had in any way caused what was happening to them, but because of his own inability to stop it, his own refusal to try and stop it.

Katrill had taken the burden of the world's survival upon his shoulders and it had become too much for him to carry. He had asked him to bear some of the burden, bear some small measure of that responsibility, but he had refused him and now it had come to this. Katrill had borne the pain of inadequacy and still strove to do his part, he had borne that responsibility like a wound that festered in his gut and spread throughout his body like a cancer.

He had asked him for help and he had responded with anger. He reflected upon all the things that passed between them, how they met, how Katrill saved his life on three separate occasions and still, he had refused to bear the responsibility that he was born to bear and in the end—Katrill had snapped. He could no longer contain his anger, his fears. In desperation and fear that he would be found too weak in the end and allow his friends to be killed, he decided to face the danger alone, and now Jodell was afraid that he would die; his only link to the power that he was heir to.

Without Katrill, all was lost because he was less than what he needed to be and had not the insight to acquire it on his own. Jodell looked up at the afternoon sky in supplication. He had never been a religious man, had never felt the need for religion. But now, he felt some strange communion, some common bond with the land that spoke of a greater consciousness, of a deeper love than even that which he still held for his lost daughter and his dead wife.

A tear perched itself in the corner of his eye as he prayed a silent prayer. "Please, God, let him be alright."

The air turned to rain. It came down in a sudden burst that caught both Jodell and Orda by surprise. It was dark and the air had been cold and still. The sky was filled with clouds, yet the stars could still be seen as they peeped through holes in the clouds. The rain came down in heavy sheets that closed off the world from either of them. Rain drops as large as pebbles pounded them, beat them toward the earth as if trying to hammer them into the ground. Water ran across Jodell's face into his eyes and mouth. It tasted old and dampened his spirit. His body shook from the added cold of the rain. He was soaked through and through and had begun to shiver but pushed on.

The rain was a torrent that washed away every feature of the landscape and colored the air a dense gray black. Jodell tied a rope around his waist and then around Orda's. It would not do for them to get separated in this storm. Jodell drank cold wine and cursed under his breath at his luck. Everything that could possibly happen was happening to stop him from getting to the Valley of Shadows. But he did not falter, though the muck sucked him in and the rain pounded at the sides of his head like millions of tiny guantleted fists. The seventh day he came to a low lying plain in the midst of the highlands.

The rain stopped as suddenly as it started. It had lasted one day and one night, and for that period of time had completely dominated Jodell's world. He had been able to see nothing but the rain, hear nothing but the rain. He had ridden in a world of silence, in a world of water that soaked more than just his clothing but his spirit as well. His determination had been diluted until all that was left was a weak watered down version of what had once been anger—anger great enough to kill by the sheer magnitude of it. The rain had beat him into submission, driven away his will to fight until he had no compunction. He was left empty like a discarded vessel.

The sky was dark, filled with huge water filled clouds, like lumbering giants marching north to some unknown battle call. Jodell watched them, his eyes glazed over like death. He had once known the exhilaration of the call of battle, the thrill of the fight. But now he was a creature of passiveness who knew nothing of such things anymore. He wanted only to close his eyes and let the earth take him, nurture him. He closed his eyes as the world began to spin and lost his grip on consciousness.

Eleven

Orda pitched camp and spread Jodell before the fire. He was leery at first, remembering what had happened only a few nights before, but there was no choice. Jodell's body temperature had dropped until his skin was cold and clammy, his color becoming an ashen grey. He had to try and keep Jodell warm until he could figure out how to help him. He poured wine, diluted with herbal medicines, down his throat by the cupfuls in a futile attempt to revive him.

He was losing the battle and Jodell was sleeping his life away. His skin turned from an ashy grey to pale white, then to a depressing shade of greyish blue. His eyes were dark grey pools and resembled burned-out coals. His breathing was slow and labored, death rattled out of his chest like the sounds of sticks beaten together for a funeral dirge.

Slowly Jodell was slipping away. Death crept up his body like slithering worms on a corpse, devouring him slowly but perceptively. Orda had done all he could do for him. He still did not quite understand what had happened to him. But there was nothing he could do so he simply waited for death to come.

Night came again and so did the rain. It fell in a light drizzle and didn't seem as cold as before. Somehow there was something different about this rain. It felt different, it felt right somehow. Orda couldn't put his finger on the difference but his senses told him that this was a natural rain, while the other had not been. Orda stretched the hide over them making a small insufficient shelter from the rain. He settled down on his blanket and watched the fire dance to some invisible tune that only it seemed able to hear.

Orda closed his eyes and tried to sleep. It was well past midnight when the rain stopped again. The clouds began to break up and the moon was trying to show itself, succeeding only intermittently. The ground was wet and small rivulets ran in every direction. The ground was covered with dead grasses which were the only thing that kept it from being a virtual mud pit.

Orda made himself a small breakfast just before dawn, packed his things and moved on. He was still heading in the general direction of south and west, with the hope of finding a healer or at least buying some medicine with which to treat Jodell. But he was worried because he hadn't much time.

By midday the low plain had turned back into hilly country and as he crested a rather large hill he spotted a small town. It was situated at the periphery of the hills where they ran into a forest. There were few people on the streets but the scent of freshly baked bread and roasted lamb drifted up to him and made his stomach ache with hunger. He descended the hill under cover of darkness and skirting the town, found a nice size clearing in the forest behind the town in which to hide their horses and Jodell. He went back to the town in search of medicines for Jodell and a fresh supply of wine.

The town was larger than it had first appeared from the top of the hill. The houses were old and in a sad state of disrepair. The streets were dirt and now had turned to mud, sucking at his shoes. It wasn't long before he came to the only tavern in the center of town. It was located in the cellar of one of the better looking buildings. A long flight of stairs led almost straight downward disappearing into darkness. Putrid air drifted up from the tavern and its patrons below could be heard at the top of the stairs laughing and shouting profanities at each other.

Orda entered. There were several doors at the bottom of the stairs, all closed except for one, where a dim yellow light glowed. The air was clogged with the heavy smoke of peat lamps and tobacco. From behind one of the closed doors someone was yelling but Orda didn't concern himself with that. He entered the smoke-filled room and took a seat. A young girl came over to him, her little green speckled eyes touched him fearfully, her lips quivered slightly as she asked for his order.

"Two flasks of your best wine and a glass," he answered her softly. She turned and walked away with her eyes on the floor. Her dress was flimsy and low cut and he could see thin lines drawn across the skin of her back. Orda wanted to ask her how she came to have those bruises but didn't. He dared not get involved, he didn't want to attract attention so he waited for his wine in the shadows of his corner. The serving girl returned shortly with two flasks and a cup. He sat for a while, poured himself a cup and downed it.

It was good wine, strong and full bodied and just slightly spiced. He poured himself another cup and sipped at it. He didn't want to call attention to himself by rushing out. He sat for an hour then prepared to leave. Just then, a huge fat man entered the tavern, there were six other men with him. He was talking loudly and hugging and kissing the young girl that had served Orda. Orda nearly shrank at the sight of him.

"The man from the inn at Dalmouth," Orda said to himself as he tried to hide his face. He eased toward the door and out. He walked like a man loaded with too much wine. When he reached the top of the stairs he let out a sigh of relief. He leaned against the door for a few seconds as his heartbeat slowed.

At the clearing he stopped and listened to make sure he had not been followed. After a few moments he entered the clearing. His stomach sank below his knees. Jodell was gone.

There were three separate tracks in the semi-muddy ground around the clearing in addition to his own. He followed them through the sparse underbrush and around the outskirts of town. The tracks led him to a back alley behind several large buildings, one he recognized as the back of the tavern he'd entered earlier. The shadows of the alley were deep and provided plenty of cover for someone surreptitiously stalking the alley. He hid himself among the shadowed doorway as he followed the tracks to the back of the tavern.

He hid himself in a doorway across the alley, watching the door and listening for noises or voices. He unstrapped his axe from its holster and stepped out into the faintly illuminated alley. The moon was full this night and gave off a faint bluish glow that painted the back of the buildings with a splash of greyed light that lent an almost depressing aura to the already gloomy surroundings. The alley was filled with garbage scattered all over the cobble stone street. Stray dogs searched through the garbage for scraps, warily searching the alley for danger and sniffing the air.

The door to the tavern opened inward, its hinges cried out like a wounded animal. The noise grated on Orda's nerves, he tensed, flattened himself against the wall of the tavern and waited.

"Tell the boss we have him and find out what his orders are," someone said to the man leaving the tavern. His voice was deep, almost guttural, with a tonic inflection that Orda recognized as the Mongodi accent. His hair raised on his neck, made him flinch. These were the same men he and Jodell had fought at the inn at Dalmouth, the same kind of men that had nearly killed them all. They were dangerous, highly skilled killers and superb fighters. He did not relish the thought of fighting them but neither could he abandon Jodell. His only chance was in taking them by surprise but even at that, he might get himself killed. But he had to chance it, he might not get another chance.

He acted. He slammed into the man standing in the doorway and at the same time, threw his axe at the second, all in one movement. The first man hit the floor, his head slamming into the stone. There was a loud crack as his skull caved in from the impact. The second man swerved to the left as he tried to dodge Orda's axe. Either he was too slow or Orda had been too fast. The axe planted itself squarely in the middle of his chest, split his heart in unequal halves. Twin streams of bright red sputtered from around the axe as the man toppled toward the floor. Orda removed his axe and headed toward a second inner door. But the short battle had alerted others from the next room and three more guards entered through the door before Orda could reach it. He turned on his heels, racing for the door he had come through. The guards moved swiftly, almost silently. A heavy blow hit Orda in the lower part of his back before he reached the door. He went down, sprawled across the body of the first man he had killed.

Orda didn't stop. He rolled with the fall, came up on his toes just in time to fend off two fast chops, one to his head, the other to his throat. He was a good fighter but could not match the speed and skill of the Mongodi. A hard palm struck him squarely in the solar plexus, knocked him through the doorway out into the alley. His head spun as the wind was knocked from him. He hit the ground hard.

He landed on his left arm, knocked all the life out of it, and lost his axe. It skidded across the cobblestones, drawing sparks like miniature stars falling from the sky, exploding against the stones. He came up on his feet again, his left arm dangling by his side like dead meat, useless to him. He would not have known it had it not been for the pain that split his shoulder and stabbed down into his near lifeless fingers. He scampered after his axe.

The alley lit up like a bolt of lightening had hit him in the face. He hit the ground again, his good arm flaying as he fell. Blood poured across the right side of his face, getting into his eyes, burning and blinding him. A gaping cut stood oozing blood just over the eyebrow where a spinning heel kick hit him.

Orda lay sprawled on his back, his vision almost completely gone in one eye, the other seeing brightly colored lights where there weren't any. He tried to get up but the world was spinning too fast and he could not get his footing. The ground heaved, rose to meet him, hit him in the chest. He vision cleared slightly. There were eight guards that formed a circle around him, watching him, their faces impassive, expressionless like unemotional killing machines. They were neither enjoying nor hating what they were doing—simply carrying out the function for which they were created.

There was a soft swish like air being blown past his ear. There was another then another. He heard voices and sounds like bones being separated. He heard low gurgling sounds like someone strangling. He forced his eye open and saw someone fall toward him. He thought he saw something protruding from his throat but couldn't be sure. He was near the edge of a great pit of fire that burned his face and chest and constricted his breathing. He couldn't keep himself from falling much longer. He cried out with his last strength hoping that the voices would prove substantial enough to help him help Jodell.

He managed to point to the open doorway to the back of the tavern. His voice was low, almost inaudible. Blood gurgled in his throat, restricted his voice, drowned his words. "My friend . . . inside . . . help."

Then he lost his grip. The pit rose up and swallowed him. He sank into the fire of his pain and lost contact with consciousness.

Twelve

Spirits danced before him, gentle swirls of feminine mists taunted him. The world was a narrow band of light that pierced the black universe. White fire burned in his chest, scorched his throat when he breathed. The light turned to water, dripping on his face, covering him, trying to drown him. He couldn't feel his arms, couldn't move his legs. His eyes didn't work, he'd lost all sense of proprioception. Only his chest moved, heaving like swells of sea waves, then relaxing, responding to the seductive moods of the moon.

He was at the seashore buried in the sand. The sun scorched his face, blanched his mind. The tide came again covering his head. Water forced its way past his dry lips, slipped down his burning throat, quenching the fire in his chest. The light died to a dull grey, receded behind the clouds and he slipped away into darkness.

"How is he?" Jodell asked as he peered into Orda's sleeping face.

"He will live. He must rest now to regain his strength. He is a very strong young man, his body fights for him and his will is strong."

"I want to thank you for saving us. We owe you our lives. I know not how I will ever repay you."

"It is not necessary to repay us. We were glad to be able to serve you. For what is love but the willing service of one person to another. In this way we show our respect for each other and all life."

Jodell eyed his rescuers quizzically and tried to respond in her manner. "Then I shall strive to be worthy of that service and repay you in kind." His rescuers bowed graciously.

The sun was setting in the west, hovering just above the horizon, painting the landscape with splashes of bright orange. Long leering shadows crept across the ground as the sun descended and the evening exerted its influence over the day.

*   *   *

Orda was up now, propped on his blankets, sipping on a cup of hot wine laced with a bitter herb tea. He grimaced at the bitterness but could feel the warmth spreading through him as he felt his strength returning. Jodell sat just opposite him, also sipping at a cup of medicine laced wine.

"How do you feel?" Jodell asked Orda. Orda looked up from his cup and smiled a weak smile.

"I may well ask the same thing of you," Jodell smiled back at him.

"You may well at that."

"However," Orda continued, "I feel fine. My strength is returning. My ribs are a little sore but otherwise, I feel fine."

"That's good," Jodell commented. "Do you think you will feel much like riding by morning?"

"I think so. At any rate, we must. We've lost too much time already." Orda finished his medicine and poured himself a cup of pure wine, drained it and poured himself another, one for himself and one for Jodell. He looked at Jodell and saw the pain in his eyes.

"Do you think he's okay," Orda asked.

"I don't know, I can't feel him."

"What happened to you back there?" Orda questioned Jodell. He had witnessed his collapse from his horse and had not been able to help him.

127

"I was attacked again. Very subtly but quite effectively. It seems that someone wants me dead very badly. And it seems that they don't intend to give up until they succeed. I'll be ready for them next time."

Jodell felt the presence of someone behind him and turned. His rescuers had been three tall women dressed in light leather riding pants and hide jackets. One seemed to be the leader, she was very dark, her color near ebony. Her hair was short cropped close to her head in very tight small curls. Her eyes were wide pools of onyx and almond shaped. She was very shapely with long legs that bowed slightly. Her lips were full, yet not large. Her small delicate-looking hands rested on the hilt of her sword which looked too large for her to handle. The other two wore their hair short also, though one wore her hair slightly longer than the others and wore a headband with the letter "H" monogrammed in its center.

Jodell motioned for them to sit and introduced them to Orda. "It's time that you met our hosts," he said as he began the introductions.

"This is Marva, leader of the group. This is Madia, the wing second, and this is the Huntress." They each bowed to Orda in turn and he to them.

It was fully dark now. The rain had since stopped, only the wet grasses told that it had ever rained. The five of them sat around the fire chatting idly, exchanging news. Only the Huntress sat unspeaking, her black eyes staring into the trees behind Jodell as she listened. She eased her bow from her shoulder and fingered an arrow that lay on the ground beside her. The others talked and laughed, downing wine and tea.

Jodell hit the ground, rolled and came up with his sword in his hand. Two arrows had swished past his head before he had time to move. He came up with the point of his sword at the hollow of the Huntress' neck.

"What the hell is going on?" he demanded as he pressed the point of his sword to her throat. A trickle of blood ran down the blade where it pricked her skin. Everything happened so fast that no one had a chance to move. Marva stood. Orda was on his feet in a second, his battle-axe in his hand, crouched in a defensive stance, ready to protect Jodell's back.

"Don't get excited," Marva spoke, her tone calm. "If she had intended to kill you, you would already be dead." Jodell lowered his sword a little and stepped back a few steps. He knew that she was right. Those arrows had come close enough to shave him and he had not even seen them, only felt the wind as they went by. He relaxed and resheathed his sword.

"What is going on?" he asked the Huntress who was now on her feet. She was the smaller of the three women and not as dark. Her complexion was a deep chestnut brown with a deep healthy glow that emminated from somewhere deep within. Her face was a small delicate affair that was highlighted by her thick black hair and her almond shaped eyes. She wore a beige suede riding tunic that hugged her bodice and accentuated her small breasts. It was tied at the waist by a brown sash with a centrally placed "H" carved out of a piece of black jade.

Marva walked over to the Huntress and spoke to her. "What is it?" The Huntress pointed to the trees across the clearing and started in that direction without speaking. The others followed her. A few feet into the forest lying in a thicket of thistle weed, lay the limp bodies of two men. Blood oozed from around the shafts of the arrows that protruded from their chests. Jodell turned to the Huntress, looked into her deep black eyes. There was a deep sorrow there, something that ate away at her, gnawing at her heart. Her eyes were sad, filled with some personal torment that she could not bear. Jodell approached her and spoke to her softly.

"I'm sorry, I didn't know. I thought you were attacking me so I reacted. I'm sorry." She did not look at him, did not answer him. Her expression remained blank. She finally looked up at Marva then turned and ran into the forest. Jodell had never met anyone like her. She was strangely compelling and he found that he liked her despite the fact that he didn't know her.

"Who were they?" Marva was saying as she bent to retrieve the arrows from the bodies.

"I saw them in the tavern when I went there yesterday. They undoubtedly work for that fat bastard," Orda said.

"Undoubtedly," Jodell echoed as he rubbed his scratchy grey streaked beard. "There is enough to worry about without having to worry about him."

"What do you plan to do?" Orda asked.

"I think we'll pay him a visit tonight and settle this."

The Huntress returned shortly with two large rabbits and a sack of pine bush and some wild garlic leaves.

Jodell and Orda ate a light meal and washed it down with tea. They waited until just before dawn then headed for the tavern.

The streets were deserted and the tavern was dark except for a single light that burned over the tavern door. It cast an eerie shadow across the building front so that the doorway was dark. They made their way to the back of the building, keeping to the shadows. The back door was open because of the damage Orda had done to it. A few boards had been nailed up against it but there was still enough room for them to slip through.

The back room was still littered with wreckage. Jodell stationed Orda at the inner door that led to the tavern proper while he went in search of the fat man. Jodell stepped into the hallway, shut the door behind him to a crack. There was a candle burning on the left wall that only marginally lit the hallway.

There was a stairway along the right wall that led to the upper level and down to the cellar. At the far end of the hall was the door to the tavern and there was another door just to the left of it. The tavern door was padlocked from the outside. The other door was slightly ajar and Jodell could hear the regular breathing of someone sleeping. There were no guards. He entered the room, drew his dagger and approached the bed.

He put his dagger to the man's throat and put his hand over his mouth. The man woke, startled. Jodell spoke, his tone deadly.

"Make one sound and I cut your tongue out while your mouth is closed. Do you understand me?" The man nodded his head frantically.

"Good," Jodell whispered close to his ear. "Now get up." The man got up slowly, he was shaking badly.

"What do you want with me? Who are . . .?"

"Shut up or I'll shut you up permanently," Jodell ordered. "We're going to visit your boss." He led the man out of the room and up the stairs. There was a guard standing outside the third room at the far end of the hall.

"Call him," Jodell commanded. The man swallowed loudly then did as he was instructed.

"Cail, come here a minute." The guard came without hesitation, happy to have a break from his guarding duty.

"What is it? What's going . . .?" His sentence was cut short as Jodell's dagger cut deeply into his throat, severing his vocal chords. He gurgled blood once then slid to the floor, heavy with death.

Jodell urged his captive on to the door. "Are there more guards around?"

"No. He was the only one," the man answered.

"If you lie to me, you will join your friend back there."

"No, please. I'm not lying, I swear. He was the only one." Jodell thought for a few seconds. He didn't trust this man, but could not afford to let him go. He did not want to kill him either, not if he didn't have to.

"Open it," Jodell ordered. He pressed the point of his blood crusted dagger into the small of the other man's back for emphasis.

"Open it!" The door opened quietly, swinging inward. The room was completely dark. A small amount of candlelight flowed through the doorway from the hall but was ineffective against the darkness inside. Jodell pushed the man in, following close behind him. There was the sound of someone sleeping very soundly, very noisily.

A faint sound to his left caught his ear, he turned his head. A blow struck him in the left eye. For a second the room lit up, bright like a conflagration of primordial power. He lashed out with his dagger, sliced from right to left. There was a howl of pain, then another blow caught his shoulder. His arm went limp, he dropped his dagger. A third blow caught him in the gut, a fourth in the chest. His breath was knocked out of him for a second, he stumbled backward against the door, slammed it shut.

The room was pitch black except for a dim red light that burned in his left eye. Hands picked him up roughly by the collar, dragged him to his feet, slammed him against the wall once, twice. His head spun. The hands released him. There was the sound of bones shattering, the deep guttural groan of death. He slid to the floor, sat there for what seemed a long time.

"You okay, Jodell? Are you alright?" Orda was bending over him, speaking to him. Blood covered one side of his face from a deep gash just above the left cheek bone. Some blood splattered the front of his shirt.

"What are you doing here? I thought I told you to stay downstairs," Jodell said, as he tried to get up.

"Yes, you did and it's a good thing I didn't. Come on, we've got to get out of here," Orda said as he dragged Jodell to his feet. He led him out of the tavern into the woods, heading for their camp.

The three women were waiting for them, their horses packed and ready to leave. They left in a hurry, the sound of excited voices at their backs. But no one followed them.

"What about the fat man?" Jodell asked Orda as they rode.

"I took care of it. We won't be bothered by him again," Jodell nodded approvingly as they rode south.

Thirteen

Jodell was still slightly woozy but otherwise unhurt. A blood-crusted cut framed his left eye, left that side of his face puffy. They rode for half a day before resting. It was late afternoon when they finally stopped. They had a light meal then moved on. Jodell's cuts were attended to by the Huntress.

By nightfall they had reached the edge of the small forest. They made camp just inside its perimeter. The trees served as shelter from the elements and also offered some amount of protection from an enemy. The leaf covered ground served to warn of anyone approaching.

The Huntress approached Jodell who sat before their small camp fire watching a pot of heating wine. She placed her small hand on his shoulder, and spoke to him. Her voice was low and musical. He had not heard her speak before and something in its quality touched him and moved him emotionally in a way he did not understand.

"It is time I changed your bandage again." She touched his head above the bandage, testing the extent of the residual swelling. He flinched a little at her touch. It sent a chill through him, unlike any chill he felt previously. His body responded to that touch with a warming sensation that started in his palms and the soles of his feet.

"I'm sorry if I hurt you," she apologized. "I didn't mean to but I must change your bandage, it's very dirty." Jodell looked up into her eyes. They radiated a deep internal warmth but at the same time spoke of some suppressed sadness that tore at her, something that she was unable or unwilling to communicate. He wanted to ask her what was wrong. He knew what self-guilt could do to you if you held it in and didn't share it with someone who would listen and understand. He knew what torment that could be living day in and day out blaming yourself for something. He understood that feeling only too well. He still blamed himself for his daughter's disappearance.

He knew the depths of that torture and the things it could drive you to do or not to do. He understood the pressure, the pain of bearing such guilt and therefore understood the need for privacy regarding that guilt.

He didn't speak to her, he simply looked at her, his grey eyes asking the question he could not yet bring himself to ask. She looked into his eyes as she finished the new bandage. He touched her arm. She looked away and moved away from him. Her voice was low and edged with emotion.

"No. Please don't." Jodell released her and she walked slowly away, moved away from him into the darkness of the forest where she could be alone. He started to stand and go after her. Marva moved to his side and touched him.

"Let her go. She is not yet ready to share her pain. Give her time." Jodell nodded and sat back down, pouring himself a cup of wine. Marva poured two cups and took one over to the Huntress. They talked long into the night.

Jodell was up to watch the sunrise over the distant hills toward the east. The sky was lighted a peach-orange and the sky itself was clear. He watched the sun rise many times before without giving it much thought. But this morning it was different somehow. There was something in the radiance that touched him. He felt younger somehow. He felt giddy, alive and exuberant. It had been a long time since he felt this way. Not since the birth of Jaecai had he felt this alive. He stood at the edge of the forest, leaned against a tree, raised his face to the sun and allowed it to wash over him. The rays penetrated his clothing, warmed him all over, driving the last vestiges of sleep and tension from his muscles.

Orda approached him, sleep still showed on his face. He stopped beside him, stretched and yawned at the sun. "Breakfast is ready if you want to eat." Jodell didn't open his eyes as he replied.

"I'm not hungry, you go ahead."

"You know," Orda said, a bit of humor in his voice. "Love does not become you."

"Am I that obvious?"

"Well, you're not exactly walking around with a sign on your back, but it's obvious for anyone who cares to notice. She is a beautiful girl, a Nubian goddess.

"Well, my friend," Orda continued. "We all have our burdens we must bear." He walked away, smiling.

Marva stepped up beside him, an understanding grin on her face. She touched his arm, startled him for an instant. He had not heard her approach.

"I could not help overhearing." She looked across the clearing to where the Huntress stood, basking herself in the warmth of the morning sun.

"She is so lovely, so totally innocent. How can one help but love her. It is not good that her young heart should need to bear such pain and guilt. One sees enough pain and misery as one gets older. To start out so young and bear such pain, it should not be." Marva turned to Jodell then, her concern for the Huntress plain in her eyes.

"Go to her, Jodell. She needs the strong shoulder of a man to cry on. Help her if you can. I don't want to lose her this way." Marva touched him gingerly on his hand. "Be gentle with her."

Jodell walked over to the Huntress. They stood and spoke with each other for a few moments, then turned and walked out of the cover of the trees into the brilliance of the sun-drenched plain. Marva looked after them. There was hope in her heart.

"Help her if you can," was all she said.

*   *   *

Jodell stood looking out across the plush green plains that stretched for miles in either direction. To the south they finally ran into the southern forest which was largely unexplored territory. The swamp lands lay beyond that and the great desert lay stretched out like a white sand blanket just beyond that.

In the middle of the desert was the entrance to the City of Leaves. He had never been to this place but heard of it through legend. Katrill had spoken about the necessity of going there, but had not said why. He would go there if he must and face whatever dangers there were to be faced in order to find the answer. But he realized that it would be difficult to find the answer because he didn't know what question he was trying to answer. Katrill had not told him why they were to go to the City of Leaves. However, he had told him why they had to go to the Valley of Shadows. They were to kill the ogre king. Thousands of human lives depended upon it. He looked out across the gentle rolling hills of the plains and contemplated his next move.

The country was beautiful. The green grass was even a different shade than that of the grasses of the north. The plain was covered with flowers, hyacinth and daisies, blue bells and Jack-in-the-Pulpit. Practically every flower imaginable was represented here.

The air was full of the sweet songs of birds, large and small, singing to their mates as they performed aerial feats that amazed and pleased Jodell and his companions. Here the earth was bountiful. Wild strawberries grew as large as man's fists and blueberries as large as pecans. Orda found a patch where melons grew as large as small logs, their juice sweet, light and refreshing. Underground streams bubbled up in different places to give ample water to the area, and here it was always spring. This was near paradise, where a man could live in harmony with nature and be at peace with himself.

Jodell sighed heavily at the thought because he knew this to be deceptive. Here, in the Valley, lurked one of the greatest dangers the world had ever known, ogres. Jodell shook his head in disappointment. Here in the truest sense of the word was Paradise Lost. He continued looking out across the plain. He had been standing there now for several hours, the sun would reach its zenith in a couple of hours. He was thinking of what he had to do. He was concerned about his companions. He could possibly make it and perhaps Orda and Marva, because she radiated that special aura of the well-seasoned warrior. But he was not sure about Media and the Huntress.

Marva approached him, disturbed his musings. "What concerns you?" she asked. Jodell looked at her, saw the determination in her eyes and knew it would be useless to ask her to stay behind.

"Look out across this country, it's so beautiful." Marva nodded her agreement. "Yet," Jodell continued, "it is the most dangerous place in all the seven kingdoms. Out there is ogres' pit, that's where I go to find my friend and complete the mission he started. But I can't allow the rest of you to risk your lives for something that doesn't even concern you. Orda and I have a personal stake in this, whereas the three of you are bystanders. I won't allow you to come with us. I will not be responsible for your deaths. I cannot bear that responsibility."

Marva placed her hand on his shoulder in understanding. She was aware of what he was going through. "As leader, I am responsible for the lives of those I command. I cannot bear that responsibility either but I do. Whenever we go into battle, I worry that one of my girls will die and I blame myself if one does. But in the end the decision is not mine. These girls have chosen of their own free will to be here and with or without me, they would still be here. My job is to keep them alive by virtue of my greater experience. If one of them is killed, it hurts the hell out of me, but I continue on. I survive. I blame myself for being inadequate but I do my best." Marva turned her back to Jodell, closed her eyes to fight back the tears of memory.

"When I left my country, we were six, now we are only three. Maybe I am responsible for the deaths of the others, I don't know. But I do know that they had the right to choose their own way and I didn't have the right to take that away from them." Marva paused to wipe at the tears that swelled in her eyes.

"Where I come from, friendship is valued above all other things. If we were to allow you to go after your friend alone and you were killed, we could never face ourselves again."

"I won't be killed," Jodell said.

"How can you be so sure of that?" she asked.

"I can't be, not really, but . . ."

"That's exactly what I mean, of course you can't. But what you can do is not deny us the right of fulfilling our responsibility to you as your friends."

Marva stepped closer to Jodell, her black eyes pleading. "Please do not leave us behind." Jodell slammed his fist into the tree he was leaning on, cursing under his breath.

"No, No, No. I'm sorry but I can't allow you to come with us. I cannot afford the guilt of more death."

Marva turned and started to walk away. She stopped a few feet away, turned and spoke, "I'm sorry, too." Then she walked away.

Another half day's ride found Jodell and Orda at the entrance to the land of the elves which was now the land of the ogres. The huge entrance was a dead spot in the midst of the lush greenery of the valley. It was a sore spot in the land, a cancer that seemed quiescent on the surface but spread throughout the land hidden from sight beneath the land's skin.

Jodell and Orda sat atop their horses at the edge of ogres' pit. The valley was drowning in a river of shadows. Already the sun was nearly gone and the sky was smeared with a fresh coat of purpled ochre. The birds had stopped their activity and nestled in for the night, while the insects were just beginning to come to life.

Everything changed when darkness came, even the scents of the daytime changed. The sweet fragrant scents of the flowers gave way to the more pungent odors of wet grass and milk weeds. The gentle chirping of the birds changed to the loud chatter of crickets and deep guttural groans of toads. The relaxing buzz of bees turned to the high-pitched whine of mosquitoes.

The night was a time totally removed from day in every respect, yet, it held just as much wonder and fascination and had its own special meaning for anyone able to feel it. Jodell had learned that appreciation. Since he met Katrill that appreciation had grown, branched into a different area.

As a sorcerer his appreciation of the night had taken on a new meaning. As a warrior he slept beneath the stars many times and sat beneath the milk-white light of the moon, had bathed himself in the pitch blackness of darkness just before dawn. But never had he appreciated the darkness on such a level as now. He understood the power, the influence that darkness had on people. He understood the hold that darkness had over the world. He understood the implications of it all and understood more than ever what his role was in it all.

He understood why Katrill had gone to all the trouble of recruiting him for this mission. He alone had the experience and drive to complete the mission. He understood the danger the Hated One posed to the world, to all the innocent children of the world. He knew now what had happened to his little girl and he could not allow that to happen to anyone else.

He came out of his reverie with a blink. Orda was watching him closely but didn't disturb him. A tear swelled in the corner of his left eye, perched itself there for a moment then rolled down his cheek to join a small pool of tears that had formed in the sink of his tense shoulder muscles. Jodell blinked his vision clear, wiped away the tear tracks from his face and urged his horse onward into the waiting darkness of ogres' pit. Orda followed closely behind.

Ogres' pit lay open to them, inviting like the open arms of a shy lover. It beckoned to be entered like the subtle urgings of a young virgin wife to her husband. The darkness spoke to Jodell. Not in words, yet still it spoke to him. "Come," it said. "Come to me and let me wrap my dark arms around you. Come and I will draw you close to my black breast and suckle you. Bring me your misty eyes and I will wipe away the dawn for I am the hand of your heart and all I touch is splendor."

Jodell nearly gave in to the temptation but fought off the lethargy that held him. He raised his head in reaffirmation of his resolve. "Come on then," he said to Orda over his shoulder as he spurred his horse onward.

They entered the pit. The darkness was thick. It wrapped itself around them, stifling them, seemingly trying to choke them. But they did not falter. They gathered their will and courage about themselves and slowly pushed back the darkness until it became nothing more than a veil of black haze.

Jodell led the way on foot. They left their horses tethered to a heavy vine just after the first turn. Their descent down was slow due to the darkness. The steep slope of the incline was treacherous.

A soft greenish glow greeted them from around the last curve. It seemed to flow around the corner hugging close to the ground but dissipating as it encountered the thick darkness. Jodell stopped and listened. Orda nearly bumped into him.

"What is it?" Orda asked. He tightened his grip on his axe. He was already sweating though it was cold in the pit. The air was musty and slightly damp and made his clothing stick to his skin.

"I'm not sure it's anything," Jodell replied. "Just doesn't feel right somehow. It's too quiet, too still." He stood for a few seconds more, listening then shrugged his shoulders and moved on.

Around the last turn they entered the main tunnel. The walls of the tunnel curved up and rounded out while the tunnel sloped downward and turned to the left. The greenish glow came from a heavy deposit of phosphorous in the cave walls and allowed enough light so that they could see.

Jodell and Orda followed the tunnel for awhile, moving slowly, carefully. Rats could be heard scampering through the tunnel behind the walls. The tunnel finally ran into a confluence of tunnels that led off in four other directions, each one twice the size of the one from which they emerged.

"Where to now?" Orda asked.

Jodell didn't answer him, he simply entered the largest of the tunnels, waving Orda forward. The grade of the tunnel decreased until they were nearly falling through it rather than walking. The air became increasingly musty as they went deeper. A slight breeze began to flow up through the tunnel as they went deeper.

Jodell moved at a pace that threatened to throw him head long down the tunnel. The faint glow of phosphorous finally gave way to a deep subtle glow like soft rush lights and illuminated the far end of the tunnel. Both Jodell and Orda stopped and listened. The grade of the tunnel had begun to level out and was now nearly flat. The air whistled as it entered the tunnel and fought its way past the rocks and up the tunnel. Jodell unsheathed his sword. Orda fastened his vestment closer to his chest after removing his axe. They both moved ahead cautiously.

The tunnel ended as a sheer cliff and emptied into another world. "Welcome to the Valley of the Shadows," Jodell said as they stood at the edge and looked out across the huge valley. Orda's breath was nearly sucked away at the beauty of what he was seeing.

The valley was an underground world. From the cliff it was a sheer drop of about a thousand feet. The floor of the valley was a series of rolling hills covered with thick vegetation. On one side was what could only be described as a forest. Huge trees grew nearly side by side; some of them so close together that they grew together to form huge misshapen objects that were at once grotesque and beautiful. The forest spread out from there, moving south and west as far as they could see. To the west there was a huge inland sea, its water, a deep blue, was still. Only a few light ripples disturbed its surface where fish came to the surface to feed. Orda could smell the saltiness in the air. Between the sea and the forest was a great expanse of lowland tundra. In the midst of the tundra was a city, a city carved out of the gut rock of the land.

The sky was the cavernous ceiling and disappeared high overhead in a thick blanket of darkness. Stalactites hung from the ceiling to the ground forming huge rock pillars that seemed to hold up the sky. The entire valley was illuminated by an unknown light source that mimicked the light of a summer moon.

"My God, this is beautiful," Orda was saying as he took in the sight before him. "I've never seen anything so beautiful."

Jodell smiled, he'd been here before many years ago when he was younger and more adventurous. In those days this was a place of peace and exceptional beauty. Those days were past now and there had been many changes. Now this was a place associated with death. The land was being neglected and going to ruin. It was not a visible ruin, not yet. It was a corruption that went deeper than the surface. It was a corruption that ate at the roots of the land and pushed it way upward. He could feel it under the soles of his feet, a cancer in the land eating it away, destroying it from within. He felt its magnitude. It was deep and malicious and he knew there was nothing he could do about it.

"He's here," Jodell spoke to Orda, his tone disturbed. Orda looked at him, saw the strained lines beneath his eyes, the tension in his shoulders.

"Where? Can we get to him? Is he still alive?" Orda asked.

"Yes, he's still alive but just barely. He hasn't much time left."

"Where is he?" Jodell paused before he answered, reaching out with his mind, trying to touch Katrill's.

"He's there, in the city. But he's weak and I can't locate him exactly. But he's there." Suddenly something cold and dark wrapped itself around his mind, pressed itself into his consciousness trying to take hold of his mind. He pulled his mind back violently, nearly lost consciousness at the effort. He stumbled and fell to his knees, nearly falling over the edge. Orda caught him, held him back from the edge.

"What's the matter, what is it?" Orda asked as he pulled him back further from the edge. Jodell blinked his eyes clear, pushed himself to his feet and stared out at the city. It had once been a fabulous city, the famed City of the Elves. But now, all the Elves were gone. Now it was a place of ruin.

"He's there. The Hated One is there. He's waiting for me." Jodell stood and rubbed his temples, rubbed at the pain in his head.

"Are you ready to face him?" Orda asked.

"Yes. I haven't any choice, do I?"

"I mean, can you beat him?" Jodell shook his head.

"Probably not."

"Then we've got to get out of here and come back when you're ready." Jodell shook his head again.

"I'm afraid I have no choice. At any rate, he'll not allow us to leave. I must fight him."

"Don't be stupid," Orda scowled. "You can't fight him if you're not ready. Jodell be sensible, it's suicide."

"Suicide or not, I must fight him. There is no other way. If you want to turn back now, it's okay, I'll understand. But I must at least make the effort. Katrill is down there somewhere and he is still alive. I can't abandon him now."

Jodell's voice dropped silently as he looked out across the valley at the desolate looking city, its streets filled with shadows and ghosts of a time past. A time when the city was alive and vibrant. Now it was a dead city, a place where death lurked, a sore spot in the face of the land. Yet it was still strikingly beautiful. There was something about the city that could not be erased. It shone through the stone, permeated the air over the city and spread out in all directions.

This too was a place of power. This city had been built by Elves and like everything else, touched by them it had a life, a power of its own that was not easily quenched. But even this power was not meant to withstand the kind of power wielded by the Hated One. His was power based on innocence so that in the end, even the ancient land of the Elves couldn't withstand him.

Jodell looked out at the city, emotion swelled in his throat, grabbed at his stomach, caused his eyes to water. The land was slowly being drained of its life. It was the last bastion of real power and soon it would be no more than a tumble of ruins hidden away from sight and there was probably nothing he could do about it.

Orda touched him on the shoulder, brought him out of his thoughts. "I understand." He reached into a bag he was carrying and produced a rope which he handed to Jodell. "Let's get going," he said. Jodell tied the rope to a small outcrop of rock and lowered the rope over the edge. He smiled at Orda then began climbing down the cliff face.

The city itself was huge. Massive towers rose into the cavernous sky terminating in spiraled peaks and golden burnished domes. The streets of the city were paved in polished marble. The walls of the city had been of massive blocks of granite, each one capped in bronze.

The walls now lay in ruin, little more than rubble and twisted metal. All that remained was the massive oak gates which stood two hundred feet tall, fifty feet wide and five feet thick. They stood on their bronze hinges, open. They were all that remained of the great elfin wall. A mute testimony to what was the glory of elfdom.

Orda and Jodell stopped outside the massive gates to stare in wonderment. "My God!" Orda exclaimed. "What happened here? Nothing human could possibly have leveled these walls." He looked around, not one block had been left intact. There wasn't a single stone left larger than a man's fist.

Jodell unsheathed his sword and dropped to one knee. He held his sword out in front of him as if offering it to someone. He bowed his head and muttered a few words under his breath, then stood, his grey eyes glistening as his face showed his emotions.

"What was that all about?" Orda asked him.

"I asked the builders of this city for their permission to enter and offered them my sword as a sign of my good intentions. It was a tradition of the Elves, it was how they showed respect for authority."

"Oh, I see." Orda unstrapped his battle-axe from its holster and repeated what he had seen Jodell do. "I don't know the words. What do I say?"

"It doesn't matter what you say," Jodell answered. "So long as the words come from the heart." Orda bowed his head, extended his axe and spoke a few words under his breath, then stood. Jodell led the way through the gates into the city.

It was getting darker as if the moon was going down in anticipation of dawn. But there was no moon so there could be no dawn. However, there was light coming from somewhere and it was getting darker, perceptively. Jodell knew it but could not worry about it. He was here to find Katrill and that was what he intended to do. He knew now that it would gain him nothing to look for the ogre king. Chances were he was already dead. The ogres were intelligent creatures; they would not have destroyed the city. Only one person could have done that and he waited for him somewhere in the city.

The light dropped to half of what it had been. The city was cast in deep shadows. The tall buildings loomed overhead and seemed to look down on them, speaking to them, warning of impending death. Jodell spoke back to them, not to the buildings but to his long gone Elfin friends. "Yes, my brothers, I shall be careful."

Orda walked beside him but didn't hear him speak. He touched Jodell more to reassure himself that he was still there than to get his attention. "Something's not right. It's too quiet. Feels like a trap," Orda said.

A slight movement caught the corner of Orda's eye. He wasn't sure he had seen anything. It seemed to be the faint glint of metal or the faint displacement of the darkness, he didn't know which.

The wind whistled behind him, a low whistle, like a missile cutting through the air. But that wasn't possible, there wasn't any wind. Orda whirled, brought his axe up in time to block the mace that sped toward his back. The force of it knocked his axe out of his hand, it skidded into the darkness. He had no time to retrieve it. He reached for the long poingard he kept strapped to his left shoulder. He heard the bones of his shoulder shatter. Pain rushed through his neck and body. His arm hung limp at his side. He closed his eyes as he dropped to his knees and waited for the next blow to end it. He heard the sound of flesh ripping, warm blood splattered over his face. He opened his eyes, trying to see. The pain that rushed into his head was too great; it blinded him.

Jodell grabbed him roughly, pulled him to his feet, pushed a dagger in his remaining hand. Orda opened his eyes, forced his vision to clear. Three bodies lay on the ground in front of him in a growing pool of thick dark liquid. The smell of blood was heavy in the air, it made him feel sick.

They were surrounded by huge dark shapes. He could not see them clearly but he could see their huge red eyes glowing like hot coals. "Ogres!" He spat out the word. His axe lay a few yards away near the foot of one of the ogres. Orda let out a yell and charged in that direction. He ducked a wide swing, the iron shod mace just missing him. He came up, buried his dagger in the belly of his opponent to the hilt then ripped sideways. He dropped to the ground grabbing his axe by the handle and in one move, swung it from left to right. He severed the ogre's leg cleanly at the knee, then charged another.

Jodell stood in a half crouch, his sword held defensively, its tip up. His entire right arm was covered in blood. A nasty wound ran the length of his arm from shoulder to wrist where he had been clawed.

Jodell's forearm was swollen to twice its size. The bone shone through at the shoulder, a deep groove in it marked where the wound began. Red marrow oozed from the wound mixed in with the oozing blood. Jodell grimaced from the pain but forced himself to all but ignore it.

Four dead ogres lay at his feet, a few others behind him. He didn't know how many he had killed, he couldn't stop to count them. All he knew was that there were more of them surrounding him, cutting him off from Orda.

For a moment the ogres watched him, red eyes boring into him trying to figure the best way to take him. He had killed many of their number. They had never met a human who could fight so well, they had learned fear but not enough. They began moving in, closing their circle around him.

Jodell screamed and charged. He could not allow them to close their circle, if he did he was done for. Better to charge them, disorient them, that way he could last longer, kill more of them before they finished him.

He swung his sword in a wide arch just at shoulder level. One, two heads flew. Warm blood covered his face, got into his eyes, blinded him. He kept swinging. He buried his sword deep in the side of the neck of another. It wedged itself between the spine and the collar bone. The ogre fell, its weight pulled the sword from his hands. Pain raced up his back from hip to shoulder. His knees buckled and he went down. A heavy blow whipped over his head, just missing. A taloned hand grabbed his throat and squeezed, lifting him off his feet.

His world spun as the lights died and darkness closed in on him. He wanted to call out to Orda to see if he was alright. His voice was strangled in his throat, spittle ran down his chin. He tried to listen, to hear the sound of Orda's axe against bone. But his ears rang with the sound of a million church

149

bells in an echo chamber. He felt his ears pop. A thin stream of blood ran from his ears and nose. He had stopped struggling. He had no more strength left with which to struggle.

He heard the whining sound of arrows cutting the air. He heard the gurgling sounds of throats filled with blood and the thud of bodies hitting the ground. Dirt muddy with blood oozed through his fingers. He forced his eyes open. He counted. One, two, no three shapes fighting, slashing a path to him. Ogres fell before Marva's onslaught. Madia covered her back while the Huntress cut them down with arrows.

It was over in minutes. He pushed himself to his knees, his right arm dangling useless. His back burned as if on fire. His throat had a band of iron around it, cranking tighter and tighter. The Huntress ran to him, embraced him. Jodell pushed at her.

"I'm fine. Orda, how is he? Help Orda."

"The others are seeing to him. Are you okay? Let me help you," the Huntress was crying, tears streaming down her face. Jodell pushed himself shakily to his feet.

"Why are you here? I thought I told you not to follow me. Damn you. You could have been killed." He screamed at her as best he could, the pain in his throat limited him.

"So could you have. If we had not followed you, you would be dead. We saved your life, doesn't that mean anything to you?" She was crying bitterly now.

"You don't understand, do you? You don't understand anything do you? You run around feeling sorry for yourself because you hesitated for a second and two people you were responsible for were killed, then you turn around and put me in the same predicament." He had her by the arms and was shaking her. "Damn you, woman, can't you see I love you. I don't want anything to happen to you. Everyone I have ever loved has died because of me. I will not be responsible for your death as well."

She looked at him, her eyes red with tears. "Oh, Jodell, I'm sorry. I . . . please, don't be angry with me. I love you so much."

"I'm sorry," he said, as he pulled her to him, hugged her tightly.

"Well, it seems we made it again doesn't it?" Orda said from behind him. "Our luck is going to run out one day, you know?" Jodell turned and clasped him around the neck.

"You're still alive, you lucky bastard." Orda winced at the pain that shot through him.

"Just barely, my friend, just barely. But I won't be if you keep squeezing me like this." Jodell released him.

"I'm sorry. My God, you look terrible."

"So do you," Orda said. They both laughed at that. Jodell stopped laughing, looked around at the bodies.

"Did we do all this?" he asked. The Huntress walked up and examined his wounds.

"With a little help from us. Come, let's attend to those wounds before they set up infection."

The Huntress waited on Jodell while Marva waited on Orda. Madia stood watch just in case. Jodell looked at the Huntress while she cleaned and dressed his arm. Her eyes met his for a second. She smiled at him.

"You were wonderful."

"What?" she asked without looking up.

"I said you were wonderful. What I saw of you anyway. I have never seen anyone shoot that fast before." She smiled up at him again.

"Thank you. It is my specialty after all."

"And Marva," he continued, "I couldn't have done better myself."

"Well, she is a swordsman. She was chosen because of her skill." She finished bandaging his talon-raked back and gave him something to fight infection.

151

"You must rest now."

"No, I can't. I must find Katrill. Then I have to find the Hated One. He waits for me."

"You can't, you must rest. At least for a couple of hours, gain some of your strength back," the Huntress protested.

Jodell pushed her gently to the side and stood on shaky legs. "It's all academic now," he said as he pointed. "It would seem I won't have to find him, he has found me instead."

A tall figure approached them. He wore a long black cowled gown. His face was hidden behind the heavy hood but his red eyes could be clearly seen.

"So we meet at last," he said as he approached them. "Good, for I'm beginning to tire of this game. It is time for an end," he spat the words out contemptuously.

"But before we conclude this little panorama, I believe you have been looking for this." He waved a long bony hand in the air. A small greenish light appeared at the tip of his finger, then drifted to the ground before them. The light began to grow and take on a shape. It shimmered for a while then coalesced into a shape, the shape of a man.

"Katrill!" Jodell called his name and bent down to him. "My God, what has he done to you?" Katrill's face was swollen to twice its original size. Blood oozed from both his nostrils as well as his ears. His chest was also swollen and moved in irregular up and down movements as he struggled to draw in each breath. Katrill half opened his eyes and managed a weak smile. He moved his lips and spoke, the words coming dry and low.

"Ah, my young friend, it is good to see you. Though I would have preferred it under different circumstances." Jodell bent closer to him, straining against the boisterous laughter of the Hated One.

"What did he do to you?" Katrill closed his eyes for a minute, his features contorting as waves of pain shot through him. He opened his eyes again. The light in his eyes dimmed, his voice lower than before. Jodell had to strain to hear him.

"It was a trap. They were waiting for me. Ogres, hundreds of them. I drained most of my strength fighting them. I guess I'm not as young as I used to be, huh." He laughed a weak laugh and was racked by a fit of coughing. He grabbed onto the front of Jodell's shirt and held on weakly.

"He was too much for me. I wasn't able to withstand him. I failed in my mission. Failed miserably as usual." Jodell wiped a tear from his eye.

"You should have waited for me, old man," Jodell told him.

"Enough of this talk," the Hated One's voice grew louder. "I could easily kill you all. However, I'm feeling especially merciful today," he grinned a toothless grin.

"I shall spare your lives if you give me what I want." He let his grin fade to a snarl. "Give me the Elf stones and I will allow you to live and become my servants."

Jodell began to rise slowly. His body began to tremble slightly as his eyes began to redden. He gathered his will behind his eyes. Katrill grabbed at him, stopped him. "No, don't. You don't stand a chance against him. He's too powerful."

"But I must at least try," Jodell said. "I don't think I have any choice."

"No," Katrill protested. "Give him the stones." Jodell knelt down again and spoke to Katrill.

"But I don't have them. We didn't go to the City of Leaves."

"No need to. You already have them."

"But I don't," Jodell said. "I don't have them."

The air lit up a dazzling hue of greenish blue as the air over Jodell's head shattered, knocking him flat. "I grow weary of waiting. Give me the stones now or you will all die, but slowly."

153

Katrill grabbed Jodell's shirt. "Your sword, check the pommel. The stones are there." Jodell went over and removed his sword from the body of a dead ogre and unscrewed the pommel. Two small rocks fell into his palm. They seemed to be ordinary rocks. He turned and threw them to the Hated One.

The Hated One filled the cavern with laughter. He held one stone in each hand. Tongues of black flame leaped into the air, lighting the entire cavern, until the ceiling of the cavern was clearly visible.

"At last, I have them, the power stones of the Elves. Now I am truly all powerful." He turned his attention to Jodell and the others and laughed a laugh of such magnitude that the entire valley shook. "Now you puny fools, prepare to die."

"Jodell," Katrill was saying. "Remember, love is the most powerful force in the universe. It is what gives meaning to life and blood is the source of life. Draw on that love that you have with your daughter for her blood calls out to you. He is hate . . . hate . . . is self . . . defeating . . . greater force . . . draw on it . . . and you will prevaiiilllll . . ."

Katrill's hand dropped from his shirt and was still. Jodell stood slowly and started walking toward the Hated One. He understood now. The Elves had entrusted the power stones to him. They knew that their power would be safe with him. They knew that they would not be around when the time came to use them. They knew like Katrill had known that he would be called upon for the task at hand. He understood that he was simply a tool used by a greater being for a purpose.

He now understood why Katrill had wanted him to give the stones to the Hated One. They were attuned to him, only he could use them. Their power would not hurt him. The Hated One could easily kill him if he used his own power, but if he drew on the power of the stones they would only drain him, leaving him weak and vulnerable.

Jodell walked toward him slowly. Red argent crackled from the corners of his eyes, spreading out around his face, framing his head. "You're a fool Jebeialle. You should not have killed my friend and you should not have killed my daughter."

The Hated One roared his contempt in a ball of blue-black fire. It hit Jodell with the force of a super nova. The explosion lit the caverns so brightly the others were blinded. The force of the explosion shook the entire plain. Rocks and stalactites rained from the cavern ceiling. The heat from the blast melted the rock beneath Jodell's feet, but did not touch him. He spread his arms and absorbed the fire. The Hated One threw another blast and another. With each successive blast he weakened, until his blasts were nothing more than small hand fires that fizzled and sputtered out at Jodell's feet.

"No!" He screamed. "This can't be happening. You must die, I cannot be defeated. No one is more powerful than I am. No one can defeat me." He grabbed Jodell's shirt, closed his eyes, and concentrated on one final attack.

A slight breeze started to blow, picking up force slowly. Soon dust was being blown in great swirls. The ground beneath their feet cracked open. Huge plumes of thick black smoke rose around them. The air above them exploded as blackish-red power erupted all around, enclosing them in a web of efferal energy. Energy pulsated from within the web, the heat was tremendous. The ground beneath them became liquid, and flowed into the cracked earth. Jebeialle's voice could still be heard above the crackle of energies as he screamed his final defiance at Jodell.

When the smoke cleared and the energies thinned, Jodell stood holding the Hated One by the front of his robes, holding him up. He spoke directly to him, power flickering from the corner of his eyes.

"No one had defeated you," he told him. "You defeated yourself when you chose to come to my house, accept my hospitality and then kill my daughter. For that alone, you must die."

Jodell let the power build behind his eyes, until his head felt swollen like a river bed at flood stage. He opened his eyes. Twin beams of red energy flowed from his eyes into Jebeialle's eyes. He let the power flow until Jebeialle's screams were lost to the sounds of Jodell's power.

Jodell closed his eyes and dropped Jebeialle's remains to the ground, a charred shell with thick black smoke issuing from its empty eye sockets. Jodell sat back for a few moments allowing his head to stop racing, letting some of his energy return. The thick smoke choked him, the smell turned his stomach.

Marva touched him on his shoulder and he turned to her. She carried the Huntress' limp, lifeless form in her arms. "She ran after you. I couldn't stop her in time. She was caught in the middle of the first blast. She died instantly. I'm sorry."

She laid the body on the ground before him. She put her arms around him and held him for a few seconds in consolation, then she walked away, leaving him to his grief.

Fourteen

The sun was high and hot. The air smelled of sunbaked grass. The air was dry and without a breeze. Though it was hot, it was somewhat refreshing after the cool dampness of the tunnels of ogres' pit. The world seemed different somehow to Jodell. Not better and not worse—just different. Perhaps it was that the world wasn't different but he was. He didn't know which and didn't want to think about it because it only made him think about what he had lost, when the Huntress died.

He started out as a simple man, forced into action because of the disappearance of his daughter, driven by rage and guilt. Now it was over and still he was filled with guilt. Except for his final obligation to Katrill, his work was done now and it was time to move on.

"Time heals all wounds, my friend." Orda walked up behind him, interrupting his musings. "In the end, even those things upon which we look at as bad, will become fond memories. Those of us who survive must do just that, survive. Life goes on, we grow old and we don't hurt so much anymore." Orda offered Jodell his good hand.

"Will you be okay, my friend?" Jodell nodded yes, and offered his hand in return.

"If it is as you say, then I will be fine."

"What will you do now, now that it's all over?" Orda asked him. Jodell looked at the sled strapped behind his horse. Katrill's body was wrapped in a clean white blanket and strapped to the sled.

"I will return his body to his order and see to it that he is properly honored."

"And then what?" Orda asked.

"I really don't know. I haven't thought that far." He wiped a drop of sweat from his forehead and fingered Katrill's staff which he'd recovered in the caverns. "I see that you have some definite plans, though."

Orda smiled at Madia who stood beside him, holding onto his arm. "Yes, I suppose I do. We will return to my city and rebuild it. We will become a nation again and a great one."

"My friends, I prepare to leave." Marva sat atop her horse, a similar sled pulled behind her. Jodell looked at the sled, his emotions clearly evident on his face. He looked at Marva.

"May I ride with you as far west as the flatlands?" he asked her.

"I would appreciate it if you did. I could use the company." Marva held her hand out to Madia in the sign of farewell. She reciprocated.

Orda watched them as they disappeared over the western horizon. A tear rolled down his cheek.

"So long, my friends," he said after they had disappeared from his sight. "Perhaps we shall meet again." Madia repeated it after him.

"Perhaps we shall, my sister, perhaps we shall."